TRUMAN CAPOTE

Breakfast at Tiffany's

Truman Capote was a native of New Orleans, where he was born on September 30, 1924. His first novel, *Other Voices, Other Rooms*, was an international literary success when first published in 1948, and accorded the author a prominent place among the writers of America's postwar generation. He sustained this position subsequently with short-story collections (*A Tree of Night*, among others), novels and novellas (*The Grass Harp* and *Breakfast at Tiffany's*), some of the best travel writing of our time (*Local Color*), profiles and reportage that appeared originally in *The New Yorker* (*The Duke in His Domain* and *The Muses Are Heard*), a true crime masterpiece (*In Cold Blood*), several short memoirs about his childhood in the South (*A Christmas Memory*, *The Thanksgiving Visitor*, and *One Christmas*), two plays (*The Grass Harp* and *House of Flowers*) and two films (*Beat the Devil* and *The Innocents*).

Mr. Capote twice won the O. Henry Memorial Short Story Prize and was a member of the National Institute of Arts and Letters. He died in August 1984, shortly before his sixtieth birthday.

BOOKS BY TRUMAN CAPOTE

Other Voices, Other Rooms

A Tree of Night

Local Color

The Grass Harp

The Muses Are Heard

Breakfast at Tiffany's

Observations (with Richard Avedon)

Selected Writings

In Cold Blood

A Christmas Memory

The Thanksgiving Visitor

The Dogs Bark

Music for Chameleons

One Christmas

Three by Truman Capote

Answered Prayers: The Unfinished Novel

A Capote Reader

Summer Crossing

Breakfast at Tiffany's
and
Three Stories

Breakfast at Tiffany's and Three Stories

TRUMAN CAPOTE

Vintage International
Vintage Books
A Division of Random House, Inc.
New York

SECOND VINTAGE INTERNATIONAL EDITION, JULY 2012

Portions of this work were originally published in *Botteghe Oscure*, *Esquire*, *Harper's Bazaar*, and *Mademoiselle*.

Library of Congress Cataloging-in-Publication Data
Capote, Truman.
[Breakfast at Tiffany's]
Breakfast at Tiffany's, a short novel and three stories / by Truman Capote—
1st Vintage International edition]
p. cm.
Contents: Breakfast at Tiffany's—House of flowers—A diamond guitar—A Christmas memory.
I. Title.
PS3505.A59A6 1993
813'.54—dc20 93-10163

Vintage ISBN: 978-0-679-74565-5

www.vintagebooks.com

Printed in the United States of America
50 49 48 47 46 45 44 43 42 41

For Jack Dunphy

CONTENTS

Breakfast at Tiffany's

1

House of Flowers

89

A Diamond Guitar

109

A Christmas Memory

125

Breakfast at Tiffany's

I AM ALWAYS DRAWN BACK to places where I have lived, the houses and their neighborhoods. For instance, there is a brownstone in the East Seventies where, during the early years of the war, I had my first New York apartment. It was one room crowded with attic furniture, a sofa and fat chairs upholstered in that itchy, particular red velvet that one associates with hot days on a train. The walls were stucco, and a color rather like tobacco-spit. Everywhere, in the bathroom too, there were prints of Roman ruins freckled brown with age. The single window looked out on a fire escape. Even so, my spirits heightened whenever I felt in my pocket the key to this apartment; with all its gloom, it still was a place of my own, the first, and my books were there, and jars of pencils to sharpen, everything I needed, so I felt, to become the writer I wanted to be.

It never occurred to me in those days to write about Holly Golightly, and probably it would not now except for a conversation I had with Joe Bell that set the whole memory of her in motion again.

Holly Golightly had been a tenant in the old brownstone; she'd occupied the apartment below mine. As for Joe Bell, he ran a bar around the corner on Lexington Avenue; he still does. Both Holly and I used to go there six, seven times a day, not for a drink, not always, but to make telephone calls: during the war a private telephone was hard to come by. Moreover, Joe Bell was good about taking messages, which in Holly's case was no small favor, for she had a tremendous many.

Of course this was a long time ago, and until last week I hadn't seen Joe Bell in several years. Off and on we'd kept in touch, and occasionally I'd stopped by his bar when passing through the neighborhood; but actually we'd never been strong friends except in as much as we were both friends of Holly Golightly. Joe Bell hasn't an easy nature, he admits it himself, he says it's because he's a bachelor and has a sour stomach. Anyone who knows him will tell you he's a hard man to talk to. Impossible if you don't share his fixations, of which Holly is one. Some others are: ice hockey, Weimaraner dogs, *Our Gal Sunday* (a soap serial he has listened to for fifteen years), and Gilbert and Sullivan—he claims to be related to one or the other, I can't remember which.

And so when, late last Tuesday afternoon, the telephone rang and I heard "Joe Bell here," I knew it must be about Holly. He didn't say so, just: "Can you rattle right over here? It's important," and there was a croak of excitement in his froggy voice.

I took a taxi in a downpour of October rain, and on my way I even thought she might be there, that I would see Holly again.

But there was no one on the premises except the proprietor. Joe Bell's is a quiet place compared to most Lexington Avenue bars. It boasts neither neon nor television. Two old mirrors reflect the weather from the streets; and behind the bar, in a niche surrounded by photographs of ice-hockey stars, there is always a large bowl of fresh flowers that Joe Bell himself arranges with matronly care. That is what he was doing when I came in.

"Naturally," he said, rooting a gladiola deep into the bowl, "naturally I wouldn't have got you over here if it wasn't I wanted your opinion. It's peculiar. A very peculiar thing has happened."

"You heard from Holly?"

He fingered a leaf, as though uncertain of how to answer. A small man with a fine head of coarse white hair, he has a bony, sloping face better suited to someone far taller; his complexion seems permanently sunburned: now it grew even redder. "I can't say exactly heard from her. I mean, I don't know. That's why I want your opinion. Let me build you a drink. Something new. They call it a White Angel," he said, mixing one-half vodka, one-half gin, no vermouth. While I drank the result, Joe Bell stood sucking on a Tums and turning over in his mind what he had to tell me. Then: "You recall a certain Mr. I. Y. Yunioshi? A gentleman from Japan."

"From California," I said, recalling Mr. Yunioshi perfectly. He's a photographer on one of the picture magazines, and when I knew him he lived in the studio apartment on the top floor of the brownstone.

"Don't go mixing me up. All I'm asking, you know who I mean? Okay. So last night who comes waltzing in here but this selfsame Mr. I. Y. Yunioshi. I haven't seen him, I guess it's over two years. And where do you think he's been those two years?"

"Africa."

Joe Bell stopped crunching on his Tums, his eyes narrowed. "So how did you know?"

"Read it in Winchell." Which I had, as a matter of fact.

He rang open his cash register, and produced a manila envelope. "Well, see did you read this in Winchell."

In the envelope were three photographs, more or less the same, though taken from different angles: a tall delicate Negro man wearing a calico skirt and with a shy, yet vain smile, displaying in his hands an odd wood sculpture, an elongated carving of a head, a girl's, her hair sleek and short as a young man's, her smooth wood eyes too large and tilted in the tapering face, her mouth wide, overdrawn, not unlike clown-lips. On a glance it resembled most primitive carving; and then it didn't, for here was the spit-image of Holly Golightly, at least as much of a likeness as a dark still thing could be.

"Now what do you make of that?" said Joe Bell, satisfied with my puzzlement.

"It looks like her."

"Listen, boy," and he slapped his hand on the bar, "it *is* her. Sure as I'm a man fit to wear britches. The little Jap knew it was her the minute he saw her."

"He saw her? In Africa?"

"Well. Just the statue there. But it comes to the same thing. Read the facts for yourself," he said, turning over one of the photographs. On the reverse was written: Wood Carving, S Tribe, Tococul, East Anglia, Christmas Day, 1956.

He said, "Here's what the Jap says," and the story was this: On Christmas day Mr. Yunioshi had passed with his camera through Tococul, a village in the tangles of nowhere and of no interest, merely a congregation of mud huts with monkeys in the yards and buzzards on the roofs. He'd decided to move on when he saw suddenly a Negro squatting in a doorway carving monkeys on a walking stick. Mr. Yunioshi was impressed and asked to see more of his work. Whereupon he was shown the carving of the girl's head: and felt, so he told Joe Bell, as if he were falling in a dream. But when he offered to buy it the Negro cupped his private parts in his hand (apparently a tender gesture, comparable to tapping one's heart) and said no. A pound of salt and ten dollars, a wristwatch and two pounds of salt and twenty dollars, nothing swayed him. Mr. Yunioshi was in all events determined to learn how the carving came to be made. It cost him his salt and his watch, and the incident was conveyed in African and pig-English and finger-talk. But it would seem that in the spring of that year a party of three white persons had appeared out of the brush riding horseback. A young woman and two men. The men, both red-eyed with fever, were forced for several weeks to stay shut and shivering in an isolated hut, while the young woman, having presently taken a fancy to the woodcarver, shared the woodcarver's mat.

"I don't credit that part," Joe Bell said squeamishly. "I know she had her ways, but I don't think she'd be up to anything as much as that."

"And then?"

"Then nothing," he shrugged. "By and by she went like she come, rode away on a horse."

"Alone, or with the two men?"

Joe Bell blinked. "With the two men, I guess. Now the Jap, he asked about her up and down the country. But nobody else had ever seen her." Then it was as if he could feel my own sense of letdown transmitting itself to him, and he wanted no part of it. "One thing you got to admit, it's the only *definite* news in I don't know how many"—he counted on his fingers: there weren't enough—"years. All I hope, I hope she's rich. She must be rich. You got to be rich to go mucking around in Africa."

"She's probably never set foot in Africa," I said, believing it; yet I could see her there, it was somewhere she would have gone. And the carved head: I looked at the photographs again.

"You know so much, where is she?"

"Dead. Or in a crazy house. Or married. I think she's married and quieted down and maybe right in this very city."

He considered a moment. "No," he said, and shook his head. "I'll tell you why. If she was in this city I'd have seen her. You take a man that likes to walk, a man like me, a man's been walking in the streets going on ten or twelve years, and all those years he's got his eye out for one person, and nobody's ever her, don't it stand to reason she's not there? I see pieces of her all the time, a flat little bottom, any skinny girl that walks fast and straight—" He paused, as though too aware of how intently I was looking at him. "You think I'm round the bend?"

"It's just that I didn't know you'd been in love with her. Not like that."

I was sorry I'd said it; it disconcerted him. He scooped up the photographs and put them back in their envelope. I looked at my watch. I hadn't any place to go, but I thought it was better to leave.

"Hold on," he said, gripping my wrist. "Sure I loved her. But it wasn't that I wanted to touch her." And he added, without smiling: "Not that I don't think about that side of things. Even at my age, and I'll be sixty-seven January ten. It's a peculiar fact—but, the older I grow, that side of things seems to be on my mind more and more. I don't remember thinking about it so much even when I was a youngster and it's every other minute. Maybe the older you grow and the less easy it is to put thought into action, maybe that's why it gets all locked up in your head and becomes a burden. Whenever I read in the paper about an old man disgracing himself, I know it's because of this burden. But"—he poured himself a jigger of whiskey and swallowed it neat—"I'll never disgrace myself. And I swear, it never crossed my mind about Holly. You can love somebody without it being like that. You keep them a stranger, a stranger who's a friend."

Two men came into the bar, and it seemed the moment to leave. Joe Bell followed me to the door. He caught my wrist again. "Do you believe it?"

"That you didn't want to touch her?"

"I mean about Africa."

At that moment I couldn't seem to remember the story, only the image of her riding away on a horse. "Anyway, she's gone."

"Yeah," he said, opening the door. "Just gone."

Outside, the rain had stopped, there was only a mist of it in the air, so I turned the corner and walked along the street where the brownstone stands. It is a street with trees that in the summer make cool patterns on the pavement; but now the leaves were yellowed and mostly down, and the rain had made them slippery, they skidded underfoot. The brownstone is midway in the block, next to a church where a blue tower-clock tolls the hours. It has been sleeked up since my day; a smart black door has replaced the old frosted glass, and gray elegant shutters frame the windows. No one I remember still lives there except Madame Sapphia Spanella, a husky coloratura who every afternoon went roller-skating in Central Park. I know she's still there because I went up the steps and looked at the mailboxes. It was one of these mailboxes that had first made me aware of Holly Golightly.

I'D BEEN LIVING IN THE house about a week when I noticed that the mailbox belonging to Apt. 2 had a name-slot fitted with a curious card. Printed, rather Cartier-formal, it read: *Miss Holiday Golightly;* and, underneath, in the corner, *Traveling.* It nagged me like a tune: *Miss Holiday Golightly, Traveling.*

One night, it was long past twelve, I woke up at the sound of Mr. Yunioshi calling down the stairs. Since he lived on the top floor, his voice fell through the whole house, exasperated and stern. "Miss Golightly! I must protest!"

The voice that came back, welling up from the bottom of the stairs, was silly-young and self-amused. "Oh, darling, I *am* sorry. I lost the goddamn key."

"You cannot go on ringing my bell. You must please, please have yourself a key made."

"But I lose them all."

"I work, I have to sleep," Mr. Yunioshi shouted. "But always you are ringing my bell . . ."

"Oh, *don't* be angry, you *dear* little man: I *won't* do it again. And if you promise not to be angry"—her voice was coming nearer, she was climbing the stairs—"I might let you take those pictures we mentioned."

By now I'd left my bed and opened the door an inch. I could hear Mr. Yunioshi's silence: hear, because it was accompanied by an audible change of breath.

"When?" he said.

The girl laughed. "Sometime," she answered, slurring the word.

"Any time," he said, and closed his door.

I went out into the hall and leaned over the banister, just enough to see without being seen. She was still on the stairs, now she reached the landing, and the ragbag colors of her boy's hair, tawny streaks, strands of albino-blond and yellow, caught the hall light. It was a warm evening, nearly summer, and she wore a slim cool black dress, black sandals, a pearl choker. For all her chic thinness, she had an almost breakfast-cereal air of health, a soap and lemon cleanness, a rough pink darkening in the cheeks. Her mouth was large, her nose upturned. A pair of dark glasses blotted out her eyes. It was a face beyond childhood, yet this side of belonging to a woman. I thought her anywhere between sixteen and thirty; as it turned out, she was shy two months of her nineteenth birthday.

She was not alone. There was a man following behind her. The way his plump hand clutched at her hip seemed somehow improper; not morally, aesthetically. He was short and vast, sun-lamped and pomaded, a man in a buttressed pin-stripe suit with a red carnation withering in the lapel. When they reached her door she rummaged her purse in search of a key, and took no notice of the fact that his thick lips were nuzzling the nape of her neck. At last, though, finding the key and opening her door, she turned to him cordially: "Bless you, darling—you were sweet to see me home."

"Hey, baby!" he said, for the door was closing in his face.

"Yes, Harry?"

"Harry was the other guy. I'm Sid. Sid Arbuck. You like me."

"I worship you, Mr. Arbuck. But good night, Mr. Arbuck."

Mr. Arbuck stared with disbelief as the door shut firmly.

"Hey, baby, let me in, baby. You like me, baby. I'm a liked guy. Didn't I pick up the check, five people, *your* friends, I never seen them before? Don't that give me the right you should like me? You like me, baby."

He tapped on the door gently, then louder; finally he took several steps back, his body hunched and lowering, as though he meant to charge it, crash it down. Instead, he plunged down the stairs, slamming a fist against the wall. Just as he reached the bottom, the door of the girl's apartment opened and she poked out her head.

"Oh, Mr. *Ar*buck . . ."

He turned back, a smile of relief oiling his face: she'd only been teasing.

"The next time a girl wants a little powder-room change," she called, not teasing at all, "take my advice, darling: *don't* give her twenty cents!"

SHE KEPT HER PROMISE TO Mr. Yunioshi; or I assume she did not ring his bell again, for in the next days she started ringing mine, sometimes at two in the morning, three and four: she had no qualms at what hour she got me out of bed to push the buzzer that released the downstairs door. As I had few friends, and none who would come around so late, I always knew that it was her. But on the first occasions of its happening, I went to my door, half-expecting bad news, a telegram; and Miss Golightly would call up: "Sorry, darling—I forgot my key."

Of course we'd never met. Though actually, on the stairs, in the street, we often came face-to-face; but she seemed not quite to see me. She was never without dark glasses, she was always well groomed, there was a consequential good taste in the plainness of her clothes, the blues and grays and lack of luster that made her, herself, shine so. One might have thought her a photographer's model, perhaps a young actress, except that it was obvious, judging from her hours, she hadn't time to be either.

Now and then I ran across her outside our neighborhood. Once a visiting relative took me to "21," and there, at a superior table, surrounded by four men, none of them Mr. Arbuck, yet all of them interchangeable with him, was Miss Golightly, idly, publicly combing her hair; and her expression, an unrealized yawn, put, by example, a dampener on the excitement I felt over dining at so swanky a place. Another night, deep in the summer, the heat of my room sent me out into the streets. I walked down Third Avenue to Fifty-first Street, where there was an antique store with an object in its window I admired: a palace of a bird cage, a mosque of minarets and bamboo rooms yearning to be filled with talkative parrots. But the price was three hundred and fifty dollars. On the way home I noticed a cab-driver crowd gathered in front of P. J. Clarke's saloon, apparently attracted there by a happy group of whiskey-eyed Australian army officers baritoning, "Waltzing Matilda." As they sang they took turns spin-dancing a girl over the cobbles under the El; and the girl, Miss Golightly, to be sure, floated round in their arms light as a scarf.

But if Miss Golightly remained unconscious of my existence, except as a doorbell convenience, I became, through the summer, rather an authority on hers. I discovered, from observing the trash-basket outside her door, that her regular reading consisted of tabloids and travel folders and astrological charts; that she smoked an esoteric cigarette called Picayunes; survived on cottage cheese and melba toast; that her vari-colored hair was somewhat self-induced. The same source made it evident that she received V-letters by the bale. They were always torn into strips like bookmarks. I used occasionally to pluck myself a bookmark in passing. *Remember* and *miss you* and *rain* and *please write* and *damn* and *goddamn* were the words that recurred most often on these slips; those, and *lonesome* and *love.*

Also, she had a cat and she played the guitar. On days when the sun was strong, she would wash her hair, and together with the cat, a red tiger-striped tom, sit out on the fire escape thumbing a guitar while her hair dried. Whenever I heard the music, I would go stand quietly by my window. She played very well, and sometimes sang too. Sang in the hoarse, breaking tones of a boy's adolescent voice. She knew all the show hits, Cole Porter and Kurt Weill; especially she liked the songs from *Oklahoma!,* which were new that summer and everywhere. But there were moments when she played songs that made you wonder where she learned them, where indeed she came from. Harsh-tender wandering tunes with words that smacked of pineywoods or prairie. One went: *Don't wanna sleep, Don't wanna die, Just wanna go a-travelin' through the pastures of the sky;* and this one seemed to gratify her the most, for often she continued it long after her hair had dried, after the sun had gone and there were lighted windows in the dusk.

But our acquaintance did not make headway until September, an evening with the first ripple-chills of autumn running through it. I'd been to a movie, come home and gone to bed with a bourbon nightcap and the newest Simenon: so much my idea of comfort that I couldn't understand a sense of unease that multiplied until I could hear my heart beating. It was a feeling I'd read about, written about, but never before experienced. The feeling of being watched. Of someone in the room. Then: an abrupt rapping at the window, a glimpse of ghostly gray: I spilled the bourbon. It was some little while before I could bring myself to open the window, and ask Miss Golightly what she wanted.

"I've got the most terrifying man downstairs," she said, stepping off the fire escape into the room. "I mean he's sweet when he isn't drunk, but let him start lapping up the vino, and oh God quel beast! If there's one thing I loathe, it's men who bite." She loosened a gray flannel robe off her shoulder to show me evidence of what happens if a man bites. The robe was all she was wearing. "I'm sorry if I frightened you. But when the beast got so tiresome I just went out the window. I think he thinks I'm in the bathroom, not that I give a damn what he thinks, the hell with him, he'll get tired, he'll go to sleep, my God he should, eight martinis before dinner and enough wine to wash an elephant. Listen, you can throw me out if you want to. I've got a gall barging in on you like this. But that fire escape was damned icy. And you looked so cozy. Like my brother Fred. We used to sleep four in a bed, and he was the only one that ever let me hug him on a cold night. By the way, do you mind if I call you Fred?" She'd come completely into the room now, and she paused there, staring at me. I'd never seen her before not wearing dark glasses, and it was obvious now that they were prescription lenses, for without them her eyes had an assessing squint, like a jeweler's. They were large eyes, a little blue, a little green, dotted with bits of brown: vari-colored, like her hair; and, like her hair, they gave out a lively warm light. "I suppose you think I'm very brazen. Or *très fou.* Or something."

"Not at all."

She seemed disappointed. "Yes, you do. Everybody does. I don't mind. It's useful."

She sat down on one of the rickety red-velvet chairs, curved her legs underneath her, and glanced round the room, her eyes puckering more pronouncedly. "How can you bear it? It's a chamber of horrors."

"Oh, you get used to anything," I said, annoyed with myself, for actually I was proud of the place.

"I don't. I'll never get used to anything. Anybody that does, they might as well be dead." Her dispraising eyes surveyed the room again. "What do you *do* here all day?"

I motioned toward a table tall with books and paper. "Write things."

"I thought writers were quite old. Of course Saroyan isn't old. I met him at a party, and really he isn't old at all. In fact," she mused, "if he'd give himself a closer shave . . . by the way, is Hemingway old?"

"In his forties, I should think."

"That's not bad. I can't get excited by a man until he's forty-two. I know this idiot girl who keeps telling me I ought to go to a head-shrinker; she says I have a father complex. Which is so much *merde.* I simply *trained* myself to like older men, and it was the smartest thing I ever did. How old is W. Somerset Maugham?"

"I'm not sure. Sixty-something."

"That's not bad. I've never been to bed with a writer. No, wait: do you know Benny Shacklett?" She frowned when I shook my head. "That's funny. He's written an awful lot of radio stuff. But quel rat. Tell me, are you a real writer?"

"It depends on what you mean by real."

"Well, darling, does anyone *buy* what you write?"

"Not yet."

"I'm going to help you," she said. "I can, too. Think of all the people I know who know people. I'm going to help you because you look like my brother Fred. Only smaller. I haven't seen him since I was fourteen, that's when I left home, and he was already six-feet-two. My other brothers were more your size, runts. It was the peanut butter that made Fred so tall. Everybody thought it was dotty, the way he gorged himself on peanut butter; he didn't care about anything in this world except horses and peanut butter. But he wasn't dotty, just sweet and vague and terribly slow; he'd been in the eighth grade three years when I ran away. Poor Fred. I wonder if the Army's generous with their peanut butter. Which reminds me, I'm starving."

I pointed to a bowl of apples, at the same time asked her how and why she'd left home so young. She looked at me blankly, and rubbed her nose, as though it tickled: a gesture, seeing often repeated, I came to recognize as a signal that one was trespassing. Like many people with a bold fondness for volunteering intimate information, anything that suggested a direct question, a pinning-down, put her on guard. She took a bite of apple, and said: "Tell me something you've written. The story part."

"That's one of the troubles. They're not the kind of stories you *can* tell."

"Too dirty?"

"Maybe I'll let you read one sometime."

"Whiskey and apples go together. Fix me a drink, darling. Then you can read me a story yourself."

Very few authors, especially the unpublished, can resist an invitation to read aloud. I made us both a drink and, settling in a chair opposite, began to read to her, my voice a little shaky with a combination of stage fright and enthusiasm: it was a new story, I'd finished it the day before, and that inevitable sense of shortcoming had not had time to develop. It was about two women who share a house, schoolteachers, one of whom, when the other becomes engaged, spreads with anonymous notes a scandal that prevents the marriage. As I read, each glimpse I stole of Holly made my heart contract. She fidgeted. She picked apart the butts in an ashtray, she mooned over her fingernails, as though longing for a file; worse, when I did seem to have her interest, there was actually a telltale frost over her eyes, as if she were wondering whether to buy a pair of shoes she'd seen in some window.

"Is that the *end?*" she asked, waking up. She floundered for something more to say. "Of course I like dykes themselves. They don't scare me a bit. But stories about dykes bore the bejesus out of me. I just can't put myself in their shoes. Well really, darling," she said, because I was clearly puzzled, "if it's not about a couple of old bull-dykes, what the hell *is* it about?"

But I was in no mood to compound the mistake of having read the story with the further embarrassment of explaining it. The same vanity that had led to such exposure, now forced me to mark her down as an insensitive, mindless show-off.

"Incidentally," she said, "do you happen to *know* any nice lesbians? I'm looking for a roommate. Well, don't laugh. I'm so disorganized, I simply can't afford a maid; and really, dykes are wonderful homemakers, they love to do all the work, you never have to bother about brooms and defrosting and sending out the laundry. I had a roommate in Hollywood, she played in Westerns, they called her the Lone Ranger; but I'll say this for her, she was better than a man around the house. Of course people couldn't help but think I must be a bit of a dyke myself. And of course I am. Everyone is: a bit. So what? That never discouraged a man yet, in fact it seems to goad them on. Look at the Lone Ranger, married twice. Usually dykes only get married once, just for the name. It seems to carry such cachet later on to be called Mrs. Something Another. That's not true!" She was staring at an alarm clock on the table. "It can't be four-thirty!"

The window was turning blue. A sunrise breeze bandied the curtains.

"What is today?"

"Thursday."

"*Thursday.*" She stood up. "My God," she said, and sat down again with a moan. "It's too gruesome."

I was tired enough not to be curious. I lay down on the bed and closed my eyes. Still it was irresistible: "What's gruesome about Thursday?"

"Nothing. Except that I can never remember when it's coming. You see, on Thursdays I have to catch the eight forty-five. They're so particular about visiting hours, so if you're there by ten that gives you an hour before the poor men eat lunch. Think of it, lunch at eleven. You *can* go at two, and I'd so much rather, but he likes me to come in the morning, he says it sets him up for the rest of the day. I've *got* to stay awake," she said, pinching her cheeks until the roses came, "there isn't time to sleep, I'd look consumptive, I'd sag like a tenement, and that wouldn't be fair: a girl can't go to Sing Sing with a green face."

"I suppose not." The anger I felt at her over my story was ebbing; she absorbed me again.

"All the visitors *do* make an effort to look their best, and it's very tender, it's sweet as hell, the way the women wear their prettiest everything, I mean the old ones and the really poor ones too, they make the dearest effort to look nice and smell nice too, and I love them for it. I love the kids too, especially the colored ones. I mean the kids the wives bring. It should be sad, seeing the kids there, but it isn't, they have ribbons in their hair and lots of shine on their shoes, you'd think there was going to be ice cream; and sometimes that's what it's like in the visitors' room, a party. Anyway it's not like the movies: you know, grim whisperings through a grille. There isn't any grille, just a counter between you and them, and the kids can stand on it to be hugged; all you have to do to kiss somebody is lean across. What I like most, they're so happy to see each other, they've saved up so much to talk about, it isn't possible to be dull, they keep laughing and holding hands. It's different afterwards," she said. "I see them on the train. They sit so quiet watching the river go by." She stretched a strand of hair to the corner of her mouth and nibbled it thoughtfully. "I'm keeping you awake. Go to sleep."

"Please. I'm interested."

"I know you are. That's why I want you to go to sleep. Because if I keep on, I'll tell you about Sally. I'm not sure that would be quite cricket." She chewed her hair silently. "They never *told* me not to tell anyone. In so many words. And it *is* funny. Maybe you could put it in a story with different names and whatnot. Listen, Fred," she said, reaching for another apple, "you've got to cross your heart and kiss your elbow—"

Perhaps contortionists can kiss their elbow; she had to accept an approximation.

"Well," she said, with a mouthful of apple, "you may have read about him in the papers. His name is Sally Tomato, and I speak Yiddish better than he speaks English; but he's a darling old man, terribly pious. He'd look like a monk if it weren't for the gold teeth; he says he prays for me every night. Of course he was never my lover; as far as that goes, I never knew him until he was already in jail. But I adore him now, after all I've been going to see him every Thursday for seven months, and I think I'd go even if he didn't pay me. This one's mushy," she said, and aimed the rest of the apple out the window. "By the way, I *did* know Sally by sight. He used to come to Joe Bell's bar, the one around the corner: never talked to anybody, just stand there, like the kind of man who lives in hotel rooms. But it's funny to remember back and realize how closely he must have been watching me, because right after they sent him up (Joe Bell showed me his picture in the paper. Blackhand. Mafia. All that mumbo jumbo: but they gave him five years) along came this telegram from a lawyer. It said to contact him immediately for information to my advantage."

"You thought somebody had left you a million?"

"Not at all. I figured Bergdorf was trying to collect. But I took the gamble and went to see this lawyer (if he *is* a lawyer, which I doubt, since he doesn't seem to have an office, just an answering service, and he always wants to meet you in Hamburg Heaven: that's because he's fat, he can eat ten hamburgers and two bowls of relish and a whole lemon meringue pie). He asked me how I'd like to cheer up a lonely old man, at the same time pick up a hundred a week. I told him look, darling, you've got the wrong Miss Golightly, I'm not a nurse that does tricks on the side. I wasn't impressed by the honorarium either; you can do as well as that on trips to the powder room: any gent with the slightest chic will give you fifty for the girl's john, and I always ask for cab fare too, that's another fifty. But then he told me his client was Sally Tomato. He said dear old Sally had long admired me *à la distance,* so wouldn't it be a good deed if I went to visit him once a week. Well, I couldn't say no: it was too romantic."

"I don't know. It doesn't sound right."

She smiled. "You think I'm lying?"

"For one thing, they can't simply let *any*one visit a prisoner."

"Oh, they don't. In fact they make quite a boring fuss. I'm supposed to be his niece."

"And it's as simple as that? For an hour's conversation he gives you a hundred dollars?"

"He doesn't, the lawyer does. Mr. O'Shaughnessy mails it to me in cash as soon as I leave the weather report."

"I think you could get into a lot of trouble," I said, and switched off a lamp; there was no need of it now, morning was in the room and pigeons were gargling on the fire escape.

"How?" she said seriously.

"There must be something in the law books about false identity. After all, you're *not* his niece. And what about this weather report?"

She patted a yawn. "But it's nothing. Just messages I leave with the answering service so Mr. O'Shaughnessy will know for sure that I've been up there. Sally tells me what to say, things like, oh, 'there's a hurricane in Cuba' and 'it's snowing in Palermo.' Don't worry, darling," she said, moving to the bed, "I've taken care of myself a long time." The morning light seemed refracted through her: as she pulled the bed covers up to my chin she gleamed like a transparent child; then she lay down beside me. "Do you mind? I only want to rest a moment. So let's don't say another word. Go to sleep."

I pretended to, I made my breathing heavy and regular. Bells in the tower of the next-door church rang the half-hour, the hour. It was six when she put her hand on my arm, a fragile touch careful not to waken. "Poor Fred," she whispered, and it seemed she was speaking to me, but she was not. "Where are you, Fred? Because it's cold. There's snow in the wind." Her cheek came to rest against my shoulder, a warm damp weight.

"Why are you crying?"

She sprang back, sat up. "Oh, for God's sake," she said, starting for the window and the fire escape, "I *hate* snoops."

THE NEXT DAY, FRIDAY, I came home to find outside my door a grand-luxe Charles & Co. basket with her card: *Miss Holiday Golightly, Traveling:* and scribbled on the back in a freakishly awkward, kindergarten hand: *Bless you darling Fred. Please forgive the other night. You were an angel about the whole thing. Mille tendresse—Holly. P.S. I won't bother you again.* I replied, *Please do,* and left this note at her door with what I could afford, a bunch of street-vendor violets. But apparently she'd meant what she said; I neither saw nor heard from her, and I gathered she'd gone so far as to obtain a downstairs key. At any rate she no longer rang my bell. I missed that; and as the days merged I began to feel toward her certain far-fetched resentments, as if I were being neglected by my closest friend. A disquieting loneliness came into my life, but it induced no hunger for friends of longer acquaintance: they seemed now like a salt-free, sugarless diet. By Wednesday thoughts of Holly, of Sing Sing and Sally Tomato, of worlds where men forked over fifty dollars for the powder room, were so constant that I couldn't work. That night I left a message in her mailbox: *Tomorrow is Thursday.* The next morning rewarded me with a second note in the play-pen script: *Bless you for reminding me. Can you stop for a drink tonight 6-ish?*

I waited until ten past six, then made myself delay five minutes more.

A creature answered the door. He smelled of cigars and Knize cologne. His shoes sported elevated heels; without these added inches, one might have taken him for a Little

Person. His bald freckled head was dwarf-big: attached to it were a pair of pointed, truly elfin ears. He had Pekingese eyes, unpitying and slightly bulged. Tufts of hair sprouted from his ears, from his nose; his jowls were gray with afternoon beard, and his handshake almost furry.

"Kid's in the shower," he said, motioning a cigar toward a sound of water hissing in another room. The room in which we stood (we were standing because there was nothing to sit on) seemed as though it were being just moved into; you expected to smell wet paint. Suitcases and unpacked crates were the only furniture. The crates served as tables. One supported the mixings of a martini; another a lamp, a Libertyphone, Holly's red cat and a bowl of yellow roses. Bookcases, covering one wall, boasted a half-shelf of literature. I warmed to the room at once, I liked its fly-by-night look.

The man cleared his throat. "You expected?"

He found my nod uncertain. His cold eyes operated on me, made neat, exploratory incisions. "A lot of characters come here, they're not expected. You know the kid long?"

"Not very."

"So you don't know the kid long?"

"I live upstairs."

The answer seemed to explain enough to relax him. "You got the same layout?"

"Much smaller."

He tapped ash on the floor. "This is a dump. This is unbelievable. But the kid don't know how to live even when she's got the dough." His speech had a jerky metallic rhythm, like a teletype. "So," he said, "what do you think: is she or ain't she?"

"Ain't she what?"

"A phony."

"I wouldn't have thought so."

"You're wrong. She is a phony. But on the other hand you're right. She isn't a phony because she's a *real* phony. She believes all this crap she believes. You can't talk her out of it. I've tried with tears running down my cheeks. Benny Polan, respected everywhere, Benny Polan tried. Benny had it on his mind to marry her, she don't go for it, Benny spent maybe thousands sending her to head-shrinkers. Even the famous one, the one can only speak German, boy, did he throw in the towel. You can't talk her out of these"—he made a fist, as though to crush an intangible—"ideas. Try it sometime. Get her to tell you some of the stuff she believes. Mind you," he said, "I like the kid. Everybody does, but there's lots that don't. I do. I sincerely like the kid. I'm sensitive, that's why. You've got to be sensitive to appreciate her: a streak of the poet. But I'll tell you the truth. You can beat your brains out for her, and she'll hand you horseshit on a platter. To give an example—who is she like you see her today? She's strictly a girl you'll read where she ends up at the bottom of a bottle of Seconals. I've seen it happen more times than you've got toes: and those kids, they weren't even nuts. She's nuts."

"But young. And with a great deal of youth ahead of her."

"If you mean future, you're wrong again. Now a couple of years back, out on the Coast, there was a time it could've been different. She had something working for her, she had them interested, she could've really rolled. But when you walk out on a thing like that, you don't walk back. Ask Luise Rainer. And Rainer was a star. Sure, Holly was no star; she never got out of the still department. But that was before *The Story of Dr. Wassell.* Then she could've really rolled. I know, see, cause I'm the guy was giving her the push." He pointed his cigar at himself. "O.J. Berman."

He expected recognition, and I didn't mind obliging him, it was all right by me, except I'd never heard of O.J. Berman. It developed that he was a Hollywood actor's agent.

"I'm the first one saw her. Out at Santa Anita. She's hanging around the track every day. I'm interested: professionally. I find out she's some jock's regular, she's living with the shrimp. I get the jock told Drop It if he don't want conversation with the vice boys: see, the kid's fifteen. But stylish: she's okay, she comes across. Even when she's wearing glasses *this* thick; even when she opens her mouth and you don't know if she's a hillbilly or an Okie or what. I still don't. My guess, nobody'll ever know where she came from. She's such a goddamn liar, maybe she don't know herself any more. But it took us a year to smooth out that accent. How we did it finally, we gave her French lessons: after she could imitate French, it wasn't so long she could imitate English. We modeled her along the Margaret Sullavan type, but she could pitch some curves of her own, people were interested, big ones, and to top it all, Benny Polan, a respected guy, Benny wants to marry her. An agent could ask for more? Then wham! *The Story of Dr. Wassell.* You see that picture? Cecil B. DeMille. Gary Cooper. Jesus. I kill myself, it's all set: they're going to test her for the part of Dr. Wassell's nurse. One of his nurses, anyway. Then wham! The phone rings." He picked a telephone out of the air and held it to his ear. "She says, this is Holly, I say honey, you sound far away, she says I'm in New York, I say what the hell are you doing in New York when it's Sunday and you got the test tomorrow? She says I'm in New York cause I've never been to New York. I say get your ass on a plane and get back here, she says I don't want it. I say what's your angle, doll? She says you got to want it to be good and I don't want it, I say well, what the hell do you want, and she says when I find out you'll be the first to know. See what I mean: horseshit on a platter."

The red cat jumped off its crate and rubbed against his leg. He lifted the cat on the toe of his shoe and gave him a toss, which was hateful of him except he seemed not aware of the cat but merely his own irritableness.

"*This* is what she wants?" he said, flinging out his arms. "A lot of characters they aren't expected? Living off tips. Running around with bums. So maybe she could marry Rusty Trawler? You should pin a medal on her for that?"

He waited, glaring.

"Sorry, I don't know him."

"You don't know Rusty Trawler, you can't know much about the kid. Bad deal," he said, his tongue clucking in his huge head. "I was hoping you maybe had influence. Could level with the kid before it's too late."

"But according to you, it already is."

He blew a smoke ring, let it fade before he smiled; the smile altered his face, made something gentle happen. "I could get it rolling again. Like I told you," he said, and now it sounded true, "I sincerely like the kid."

"What scandals are you spreading, O.J.?" Holly splashed into the room, a towel more or less wrapped round her and her wet feet dripping footmarks on the floor.

"Just the usual. That you're nuts."

"Fred knows that already."

"But you don't."

"Light me a cigarette, darling," she said, snatching off a bathing cap and shaking her hair. "I don't mean you, O.J. You're such a slob. You always nigger-lip."

She scooped up the cat and swung him onto her shoulder. He perched there with the balance of a bird, his paws tangled in her hair as if it were knitting yarn; and yet, despite these amiable antics, it was a grim cat with a pirate's cutthroat face; one eye was gluey-blind, the other sparkled with dark deeds.

"O.J. is a slob," she told me, taking the cigarette I'd lighted. "But he does know a terrific lot of phone numbers. What's David O. Selznick's number, O.J.?"

"Lay off."

"It's not a joke, darling. I want you to call him up and tell him what a genius Fred is. He's written barrels of the most marvelous stories. Well, don't blush, Fred: you didn't say you were a genius, I did. Come on, O.J. What are you going to do to make Fred rich?"

"Suppose you let me settle that with Fred."

"Remember," she said, leaving us, "I'm his agent. Another thing: if I holler, come zipper me up. And if anybody knocks, let them in."

A multitude did. Within the next quarter-hour a stag party had taken over the apartment, several of them in uniform. I counted two Naval officers and an Air Force colonel; but they were outnumbered by graying arrivals beyond draft status. Except for a lack of youth, the guests had no common theme, they seemed strangers among strangers; indeed, each face, on entering, had struggled to conceal dismay at seeing others there. It was as if the hostess had distributed her invitations while zigzagging through various bars; which was probably the case. After the initial frowns, however, they mixed without grumbling, especially O.J. Berman, who avidly exploited the new company to avoid discussing my Hollywood future. I was left abandoned by the bookshelves; of the books there, more than half were about horses, the rest baseball. Pretending an interest in *Horseflesh and How to Tell It* gave me sufficiently private opportunity for sizing Holly's friends.

Presently one of these became prominent. He was a middle-aged child that had never shed its baby fat, though some gifted tailor had almost succeeded in camouflaging his plump and spankable bottom. There wasn't a suspicion of bone in his body; his face, a zero filled in with pretty miniature features, had an unused, a virginal quality: it was as if he'd been born, then expanded, his skin remaining unlined as a blown-up balloon, and his mouth, though ready for squalls and tantrums, a spoiled sweet puckering. But it was not appearance that singled him out; preserved infants aren't all that rare. It was, rather, his conduct; for he was behaving as though the party were his: like an energetic octopus, he was shaking martinis, making introductions, manipulating the phonograph. In fairness, most of his activities were dictated by the hostess herself: *Rusty, would you mind; Rusty, would you please.* If he was in love with her, then clearly he had his jealousy in check. A jealous man might have lost control, watching her as she skimmed around the room, carrying her cat in one hand but leaving the other free to straighten a tie or remove lapel lint; the Air Force colonel wore a medal that came in for quite a polish.

The man's name was Rutherfurd ("Rusty") Trawler. In 1908 he'd lost both his parents, his father the victim of an anarchist and his mother of shock, which double misfortune had made Rusty an orphan, a millionaire, and a celebrity, all at the age of five. He'd been a stand-by of the Sunday supplements ever since, a consequence that had gathered hurricane momentum when, still a schoolboy, he had caused his godfather-custodian to be arrested on charges of sodomy. After that, marriage and divorce sustained his place in the tabloid-sun. His first wife had taken herself, and her alimony, to a rival of Father Divine's. The second wife seems unaccounted for, but the third had sued him in New York State with a full satchel of the kind of testimony that entails. He himself divorced the last Mrs. Trawler, his principal complaint stating that she'd started a mutiny aboard his yacht, said mutiny resulting in his being deposited on the Dry Tortugas. Though he'd been a bachelor since, apparently before the war he'd proposed to Unity Mitford, at least he was supposed to have sent her a cable offering to marry her if Hitler didn't. This was said to be the reason Winchell always referred to him as a Nazi; that, and the fact that he attended rallies in Yorkville.

I was not told these things. I read them in *The Baseball Guide,* another selection off Holly's shelf which she seemed to use for a scrapbook. Tucked between the pages were Sunday features, together with scissored snippings from gossip columns. *Rusty Trawler and Holly Golightly two-on-the-aisle at "One Touch of Venus" preem.* Holly came up from behind, and caught me reading: *Miss Holiday Golightly, of the Boston Golightlys, making every day a holiday for the 24-karat Rusty Trawler.*

"Admiring my publicity, or are you just a baseball fan?" she said, adjusting her dark glasses as she glanced over my shoulder.

I said, "What was this week's weather report?"

She winked at me, but it was humorless: a wink of warning, "I'm all for horses, but I loathe baseball," she said, and the sub-message in her voice was saying she wished me to forget she'd ever mentioned Sally Tomato. "I hate the sound of it on a radio, but I have to listen, it's part of my research. There're so few things men can talk about. If a man doesn't like baseball, then he must like horses, and if he doesn't like either of them, well, I'm in trouble anyway: he don't like girls. And how are you making out with O.J.?"

"We've separated by mutual agreement."

"He's an opportunity, believe me."

"I do believe you. But what have I to offer that would strike him as an opportunity?"

She persisted. "Go over there and make him think he isn't funny-looking. He really can help you, Fred."

"I understand you weren't too appreciative." She seemed puzzled until I said: "*The Story of Doctor Wassell.*"

"He's still harping?" she said, and cast across the room an affectionate look at Berman. "But he's got a point, I *should* feel guilty. Not because they would have given me the part or because I would have been good: they wouldn't and I wouldn't. If I do feel guilty, I guess it's because I let him go on dreaming when I wasn't dreaming a bit. I was just vamping for time to make a few self-improvements: I knew damn well I'd never be a movie star. It's too hard; and if you're intelligent, it's too embarrassing. My complexes aren't inferior enough: being a movie star and having a big fat ego are supposed to go hand-in-hand; actually, it's essential not to have any ego at all. I don't mean I'd mind being rich and famous. That's very much on my schedule, and someday I'll try to get around to it; but if it happens, I'd like to have my ego tagging along. I want to still be me when I wake up one fine morning and have breakfast at Tiffany's. You need a glass," she said, noticing my empty hands. "Rusty! Will you bring my friend a drink?"

She was still hugging the cat. "Poor slob," she said, tickling his head, "poor slob without a name. It's a little inconvenient, his not having a name. But I haven't any right to give him one: he'll have to wait until he *belongs* to somebody. We just sort of took up by the river one day, we don't belong to each other: he's an independent, and so am I. I don't want to own anything until I know I've found the place where me and things belong together. I'm not quite sure where that is just yet. But I know what it's like." She smiled, and let the cat drop to the floor. "It's like Tiffany's," she said. "Not that I give a hoot about jewelry. Diamonds, yes. But it's tacky to wear diamonds before you're forty; and even that's risky. They only look right on the really old girls. Maria Ouspenskaya. Wrinkles and bones, white hair and diamonds: I can't wait. But that's not why I'm mad about Tiffany's. Listen. You know those days when you've got the mean reds?"

"Same as the blues?"

"No," she said slowly. "No, the blues are because you're getting fat or maybe it's been raining too long. You're sad, that's all. But the mean reds are horrible. You're afraid and you sweat like hell, but you don't know what you're afraid of. Except something bad is going to happen, only you don't know what it is. You've had that feeling?"

"Quite often. Some people call it *angst*."

"All right. *Angst*. But what do you do about it?"

"Well, a drink helps."

"I've tried that. I've tried aspirin, too. Rusty thinks I should smoke marijuana, and I did for a while, but it only makes me giggle. What I've found does the most good is just to get into a taxi and go to Tiffany's. It calms me down right away, the quietness and the proud look of it; nothing very bad could happen to you there, not with those kind men in their nice suits, and that lovely smell of silver and alligator wallets. If I could find a real-life place that made me feel like Tiffany's, then I'd buy some furniture and give the cat a name. I've thought maybe after the war, Fred and I—" She pushed up her dark glasses, and her eyes, the differing colors of them, the grays and wisps of blue and green, had taken on a far-seeing sharpness. "I went to Mexico once. It's wonderful country for raising horses. I saw one place near the sea. Fred's good with horses."

Rusty Trawler came carrying a martini; he handed it over without looking at me. "I'm hungry," he announced, and his voice, retarded as the rest of him, produced an unnerving brat-whine that seemed to blame Holly. "It's seven-thirty, and I'm hungry. You know what the doctor said."

"Yes, Rusty. I know what the doctor said."

"Well, then break it up. Let's go."

"I want you to behave, Rusty." She spoke softly, but there was a governess threat of punishment in her tone that caused an odd flush of pleasure, of gratitude, to pink his face.

"You don't love me," he complained, as though they were alone.

"Nobody loves naughtiness."

Obviously she'd said what he wanted to hear; it appeared to both excite and relax him. Still he continued, as though it were a ritual: "Do you love me?"

She patted him. "Tend to your chores, Rusty. And when I'm ready, we'll go eat wherever you want."

"Chinatown?"

"But that doesn't mean sweet and sour spareribs. You know what the doctor said."

As he returned to his duties with a satisfied waddle, I couldn't resist reminding her that she hadn't answered his question. "*Do* you love him?"

"I told you: you can make yourself love anybody. Besides, he had a stinking childhood."

"If it was so stinking, why does he cling to it?"

"Use your head. Can't you see it's just that Rusty feels

safer in diapers than he would in a skirt? Which is really the choice, only he's awfully touchy about it. He tried to stab me with a butter knife because I told him to grow up and face the issue, settle down and play house with a nice fatherly truck driver. Meantime, I've got him on my hands; which is okay, he's harmless, he thinks girls are dolls literally."

"Thank God."

"Well, if it were true of most men, I'd hardly be thanking God."

"I meant thank God you're not going to marry Mr. Trawler."

She lifted an eyebrow. "By the way, I'm not pretending I don't know he's rich. Even land in Mexico costs something. Now," she said, motioning me forward, "let's get hold of O.J."

I held back while my mind worked to win a postponement. Then I remembered: "Why *Traveling?*"

"On my card?" she said, disconcerted. "You think it's funny?"

"Not funny. Just provocative."

She shrugged. "After all, how do I know where I'll be living tomorrow? So I told them to put *Traveling.* Anyway, it was a waste of money, ordering those cards. Except I felt I owed it to them to buy some little *some*thing. They're from Tiffany's." She reached for my martini, I hadn't touched it; she drained it in two swallows, and took my hand. "Quit stalling. You're going to make friends with O.J."

An occurrence at the door intervened. It was a young woman, and she entered like a wind-rush, a squall of scarves and jangling gold. "H-H-Holly," she said, wagging a finger as she advanced, "you miserable h-h-hoarder. Hogging all these simply r-r-riveting m-m-men!"

She was well over six feet, taller than most men there.

They straightened their spines, sucked in their stomachs; there was a general contest to match her swaying height.

Holly said, "What are you doing here?" and her lips were taut as drawn string.

"Why, n-n-nothing, sugar. I've been upstairs working with Yunioshi. Christmas stuff for the *Ba-ba-zaar.* But you sound vexed, sugar?" She scattered a roundabout smile. "You b-b-boys not vexed at me for butting in on your p-p-party?"

Rusty Trawler tittered. He squeezed her arm, as though to admire her muscle, and asked her if she could use a drink.

"I surely could," she said. "Make mine bourbon."

Holly told her, "There *isn't* any." Whereupon the Air Force colonel suggested he run out for a bottle.

"Oh, I declare, don't let's have a f-f-fuss. I'm happy with ammonia. Holly, honey," she said, slightly shoving her, "don't you bother about me. I can introduce myself." She stooped toward O.J. Berman, who, like many short men in the presence of tall women, had an aspiring mist in his eye. "I'm Mag W-w-wildwood, from Wild-w-w-wood, Arkansas. That's hill country."

It seemed a dance, Berman performing some fancy footwork to prevent his rivals cutting in. He lost her to a quadrille of partners who gobbled up her stammered jokes like popcorn tossed to pigeons. It was a comprehensible success. She was a triumph over ugliness, so often more beguiling than real beauty, if only because it contains paradox. In this case, as opposed to the scrupulous method of plain good taste and scientific grooming, the trick had been worked by exaggerating defects; she'd made them ornamental by admitting them boldly. Heels that emphasized her height, so steep her ankles trembled; a flat tight bodice that indicated she could go to a beach in bathing trunks; hair that was pulled straight back, accentuating the spareness, the starvation of her fashion-model face. Even the stutter, certainly genuine but still a bit laid on, had been turned to advantage. It was the master stroke, that stutter; for it contrived to make her banalities sound somehow original, and secondly, despite her tallness, her assurance, it served to inspire in male listeners a protective feeling. To illustrate: Berman had to be pounded on the back because she said, "Who can tell me w-w-where is the j-j-john?"; then, completing the cycle, he offered an arm to guide her himself.

"That," said Holly, "won't be necessary. She's been here before. She knows where it is." She was emptying ashtrays, and after Mag Wildwood had left the room, she emptied another, then said, sighed rather: "It's really very sad." She paused long enough to calculate the number of inquiring expressions; it was sufficient. "And so mysterious. You'd think it would show more. But heaven knows, she *looks* healthy. So, well, *clean*. That's the extraordinary part. Wouldn't you," she asked with concern, but of no one in particular, "wouldn't you say she *looked* clean?"

Someone coughed, several swallowed. A Naval officer, who had been holding Mag Wildwood's drink, put it down.

"But then," said Holly, "I hear so many of these Southern girls have the same trouble." She shuddered delicately, and went to the kitchen for more ice.

Mag Wildwood couldn't understand it, the abrupt absence of warmth on her return; the conversations she began behaved like green logs, they fumed but would not fire. More unforgivably, people were leaving without taking her telephone number. The Air Force colonel decamped while her back was turned, and this was the straw too much: he'd asked her to dinner. Suddenly she was blind. And since gin to artifice bears the same relation as tears to mascara, her attractions at once dissembled. She took it out on everyone. She called her hostess a Hollywood degenerate. She invited a man in his fifties to fight. She told Berman, Hitler was right. She exhilarated Rusty Trawler by stiff-arming him into a corner. "You know what's going to happen to you?" she said, with no hint of a stutter. "I'm going to march you over to the zoo and feed you to the yak." He looked altogether willing, but she disappointed him by sliding to the floor, where she sat humming.

"You're a bore. Get up from there," Holly said, stretching on a pair of gloves. The remnants of the party were waiting at the door, and when the bore didn't budge Holly cast me an apologetic glance. "Be an angel, would you, Fred? Put her in a taxi. She lives at the Winslow."

"Don't. Live Barbizon. Regent 4-5700. Ask for Mag Wildwood."

"You *are* an angel, Fred."

They were gone. The prospect of steering an Amazon into a taxi obliterated whatever resentment I felt. But she solved the problem herself. Rising on her own steam, she stared down at me with a lurching loftiness. She said, "Let's go Stork. Catch lucky balloon," and fell full-length like an axed oak. My first thought was to run for a doctor. But examination proved her pulse fine and her breathing regular. She was simply asleep. After finding a pillow for her head, I left her to enjoy it.

THE FOLLOWING AFTERNOON I COLLIDED with Holly on the stairs. *"You"* she said, hurrying past with a package from the druggist. "There she is, on the verge of pneumonia. A hang-over out to here. And the mean reds on top of it." I gathered from this that Mag Wildwood was still in the apartment, but she gave me no chance to explore her surprising sympathy. Over the weekend, mystery deepened. First, there was the Latin who came to my door: mistakenly, for he was inquiring after Miss Wildwood. It took a while to correct his error, our accents seemed mutually incoherent, but by the time we had I was charmed. He'd been put together with care, his brown head and bullfighter's figure had an exactness, a perfection, like an apple, an orange, something nature has made just right. Added to this, as decoration, were an English suit and a brisk cologne and, what is still more unlatin, a bashful manner. The second event of the day involved him again. It was toward evening, and I saw him on my way out to dinner. He was arriving in a taxi; the driver helped him totter into the house with a load of suitcases. That gave me something to chew on: by Sunday my jaws were quite tired.

Then the picture became both darker and clearer.

Sunday was an Indian summer day, the sun was strong, my window was open, and I heard voices on the fire escape. Holly and Mag were sprawled there on a blanket, the cat between them. Their hair, newly washed, hung lankly. They were busy, Holly varnishing her toenails, Mag knitting on a sweater. Mag was speaking.

"If you ask me, I think you're l-l-lucky. At least there's one thing you can say for Rusty. He's an American."

"Bully for him."

"*Sugar.* There's a war on."

"And when it's over, you've seen the last of me, boy."

"I don't feel that way. I'm p-p-proud of my country. The men in my family were great soldiers. There's a statue of Papadaddy Wildwood smack in the center of Wildwood."

"Fred's a soldier," said Holly. "But I doubt if he'll ever

be a statue. Could be. They say the more stupid you are the braver. He's pretty stupid."

"Fred's that boy upstairs? I didn't realize he was a soldier. But he *does* look stupid."

"Yearning. Not stupid. He wants awfully to be on the inside staring out: anybody with their nose pressed against a glass is liable to look stupid. Anyhow, he's a different Fred. Fred's my brother."

"You call your own f-f-flesh and b-b-blood stupid?"

"If he is he is."

"Well, it's poor taste to say so. A boy that's fighting for you and me and all of us."

"What is this: a bond rally?"

"I just want you to know where I stand. I appreciate a joke, but underneath I'm a s-s-serious person. Proud to be an American. That's why I'm sorry about José." She put down her knitting needles. "You *do* think he's terribly good-looking, don't you?" Holly said Hmn, and swiped the cat's whiskers with her lacquer brush. "If only I could get used to the idea of m-m marrying a Brazilian. And *being* a B-b-brazilian myself. It's such a canyon to cross. Six thousand miles, and not knowing the language—"

"Go to Berlitz."

"Why on earth would they be teaching P-p-portuguese? It isn't as though anyone spoke it. No, my only chance is to try and make José forget politics and become an American. It's such a useless thing for a man to want to be: the p-p-president of *Brazil.*" She sighed and picked up her knitting. "I must be madly in love. You saw us together. Do you think I'm madly in love?"

"Well. Does he bite?"

Mag dropped a stitch. "Bite?"

"You. In bed."

"Why, no. *Should* he?" Then she added, censoriously: "But he does laugh."

"Good. That's the right spirit. I like a man who sees the humor; most of them, they're all pant and puff."

Mag withdrew her complaint; she accepted the comment as flattery reflecting on herself. "Yes. I suppose."

"Okay. He doesn't bite. He laughs. What else?"

Mag counted up her dropped stitch and began again, knit, purl, purl.

"I said—"

"I heard you. And it isn't that I don't want to tell you. But it's so difficult to remember. I don't d-d-dwell on these things. The way you seem to. They go out of my head like a dream. I'm sure that's the n-n-normal attitude."

"It may be normal, darling; but I'd rather be natural." Holly paused in the process of reddening the rest of the cat's whiskers. "Listen. If you can't remember, try leaving the lights on."

"Please understand me, Holly. I'm a very-very-very *conventional* person."

"Oh, balls. What's wrong with a decent look at a guy you like? Men are beautiful, a lot of them are, José is, and if you don't even want to *look* at him, well, I'd say he's getting a pretty cold plate of macaroni."

"L-l-lower your voice."

"You can't possibly be in love with him. Now. Does that answer your question?"

"No. Because I'm not a cold plate of m-m-macaroni. I'm a warm-hearted person. It's the basis of my character."

"Okay. You've got a warm heart. But if I were a man on my way to bed, I'd rather take along a hot-water bottle. It's more tangible."

"You won't hear any squawks out of José," she said complacently, her needles flashing in the sunlight. "What's more, I *am* in love with him. Do you realize I've knitted ten pairs of Argyles in less than three months? And this is the second sweater." She stretched the sweater and tossed it aside. "What's the point, though? Sweaters in Brazil. I ought to be making s-s-sun helmets."

Holly lay back and yawned. "It must be winter sometime."

"It *rains,* that I know. Heat. Rain. J-j-jungles."

"Heat. Jungles. Actually, I'd like that."

"Better you than me."

"Yes," said Holly, with a sleepiness that was not sleepy. "Better me than you."

ON MONDAY, WHEN I WENT down for the morning mail, the card on Holly's box had been altered, a name added: Miss Golightly and Miss Wildwood were now traveling together. This might have held my interest longer except for a letter in my own mailbox. It was from a small university review to whom I'd sent a story. They liked it; and, though I must understand they could not afford to pay, they intended to publish. Publish: that meant *print.* Dizzy with excitement is no mere phrase. I had to tell someone: and, taking the stairs two at a time, I pounded on Holly's door.

I didn't trust my voice to tell the news; as soon as she came to the door, her eyes squinty with sleep, I thrust the letter at her. It seemed as though she'd had time to read sixty pages before she handed it back. "I wouldn't let them do it, not if they don't pay you," she said, yawning. Perhaps my face explained she'd misconstrued, that I'd not wanted advice but congratulations: her mouth shifted from a yawn into a smile. "Oh, I see. It's wonderful. Well, come in," she said. "We'll make a pot of coffee and celebrate. No. I'll get dressed and take you to lunch."

Her bedroom was consistent with her parlor: it perpetuated the same camping-out atmosphere; crates and suitcases, everything packed and ready to go, like the belongings of a criminal who feels the law not far behind. In the parlor there was no conventional furniture, but the bedroom had the bed itself, a double one at that, and quite flashy: blond wood, tufted satin.

She left the door of the bathroom open, and conversed from there; between the flushing and the brushing, most of what she said was unintelligible, but the gist of it was: she *supposed* I knew Mag Wildwood had moved in, and wasn't that *convenient?* because if you're going to *have* a roommate, and she *isn't* a dyke, then the next best thing is a *perfect* fool, which Mag *was,* because then you can dump the lease on them *and* send them out for the laundry.

One could see that Holly had a laundry problem; the room was strewn, like a girl's gymnasium.

"—and you know, she's quite a successful model: isn't that *fantastic*? But a good thing," she said, hobbling out of the bathroom as she adjusted a garter. "It ought to keep her out of my hair most of the day. And there shouldn't be too much trouble on the man front. She's engaged. Nice guy, too. Though there's a tiny difference in height: I'd say a foot, her favor. Where the hell—" She was on her knees poking under the bed. After she'd found what she was looking for, a pair of lizard shoes, she had to search for a blouse, a belt, and it was a subject to ponder, how, from such wreckage, she evolved the eventual effect: pampered, calmly immaculate, as though she'd been attended by Cleopatra's maids. She said, "Listen," and cupped her hand under my chin, "I'm glad about the story. Really I am."

THAT MONDAY IN OCTOBER, 1943. A beautiful day with the buoyancy of a bird. To start, we had Manhattans at Joe Bell's; and, when he heard of my good luck, champagne cocktails on the house. Later, we wandered toward Fifth Avenue, where there was a parade. The flags in the wind, the thump of military bands and military feet, seemed to have nothing to do with war, but to be, rather, a fanfare arranged in my personal honor.

We ate lunch at the cafeteria in the park. Afterwards, avoiding the zoo (Holly said she couldn't bear to see anything in a cage), we giggled, ran, sang along the paths toward the old wooden boathouse, now gone. Leaves floated on the lake; on the shore, a park-man was fanning a bonfire of them, and the smoke, rising like Indian signals, was the only smudge on the quivering air. Aprils have never meant much to me, autumns seem that season of beginning, spring; which is how I felt sitting with Holly on the railings of the boathouse porch. I thought of the future, and spoke of the past. Because Holly wanted to know about my childhood. She talked of her own, too; but it was elusive, nameless, placeless, an impressionistic recital, though the impression received was contrary to what one expected, for she gave an almost voluptuous account of swimming and summer, Christmas trees, pretty cousins and parties: in short, happy in a way that she was not, and never, certainly, the background of a child who had run away.

Or, I asked, wasn't it true that she'd been out on her own

since she was fourteen? She rubbed her nose. "That's true. The other isn't. But really, darling, you made such a tragedy out of *your* childhood I didn't feel I should compete."

She hopped off the railing. "Anyway, it reminds me: I ought to send Fred some peanut butter." The rest of the afternoon we were east and west worming out of reluctant grocers cans of peanut butter, a wartime scarcity; dark came before we'd rounded up a half-dozen jars, the last at a delicatessen on Third Avenue. It was near the antique shop with the palace of a bird cage in its window, so I took her there to see it, and she enjoyed the point, its fantasy: "But still, it's a cage."

Passing a Woolworth's, she gripped my arm: "Let's steal something," she said, pulling me into the store, where at once there seemed a pressure of eyes, as though we were already under suspicion. "Come on. Don't be chicken." She scouted a counter piled with paper pumpkins and Halloween masks. The saleslady was occupied with a group of nuns who were trying on masks. Holly picked up a mask and slipped it over her face; she chose another and put it on mine; then she took my hand and we walked away. It was as simple as that. Outside, we ran a few blocks, I think to make it more dramatic; but also because, as I'd discovered, successful theft exhilarates. I wondered if she'd often stolen. "I used to," she said. "I mean I had to. If I wanted anything. But I still do it every now and then, sort of to keep my hand in."

We wore the masks all the way home.

I HAVE A MEMORY OF spending many hither and yonning days with Holly; and it's true, we did at odd moments see a great deal of each other; but on the whole, the memory is false. Because toward the end of the month I found a job: what is there to add? The less the better, except to say it was necessary and lasted from nine to five. Which made our hours, Holly's and mine, extremely different.

Unless it was Thursday, her Sing Sing day, or unless she'd gone horseback riding in the park, as she did occasionally, Holly was hardly up when I came home. Sometimes, stopping there, I shared her wake-up coffee while she dressed for the evening. She was forever on her way out, not always with Rusty Trawler, but usually, and usually, too, they were joined by Mag Wildwood and the handsome Brazilian, whose name was José Ybarra-Jaegar: his mother was German. As a quartet, they struck an unmusical note, primarily the fault of Ybarra-Jaegar, who seemed as out of place in their company as a violin in a jazz band. He was intelligent, he was presentable, he appeared to have a serious link with his work, which was obscurely governmental, vaguely important, and took him to Washington several days a week. How, then, could he survive night after night in La Rue, El Morocco, listening to the Wildwood ch-ch-chatter and staring into Rusty's raw baby-buttocks face? Perhaps, like most of us in a foreign country, he was incapable of placing people, selecting a frame for their picture, as he would at home; therefore all Americans had to be judged in a pretty equal light, and on this basis his companions appeared to be tolerable examples of local color and national character. That would explain much; Holly's determination explains the rest.

Late one afternoon, while waiting for a Fifth Avenue bus, I noticed a taxi stop across the street to let out a girl who ran up the steps of the Forty-second Street public library. She was through the doors before I recognized her, which was pardonable, for Holly and libraries were not an easy association to make. I let curiosity guide me between the lions, debating on the way whether I should admit following her or pretend coincidence. In the end I did neither, but concealed myself some tables away from her in the general reading room, where she sat behind her dark glasses and a fortress of literature she'd gathered at the desk. She sped from one book to the next, intermittently lingering on a page, always with a frown, as if it were printed upside down. She had a pencil poised above paper—nothing seemed to catch her fancy, still now and then, as though for the hell of it, she made laborious scribblings. Watching her, I remembered a girl I'd known in school, a grind, Mildred Grossman. Mildred: with her moist hair and greasy spectacles, her stained fingers that dissected frogs and carried coffee to picket lines, her flat eyes that only turned toward the stars to estimate their chemical tonnage. Earth and air could not be more opposite than Mildred and Holly, yet in my head they acquired a Siamese twinship, and the thread of thought that had sewn them together ran like this: the average personality reshapes frequently, every few years even our bodies undergo a complete overhaul—desirable or not, it is a natural thing that we should change. All right, here were two people who never would. That is what Mildred Grossman had in common with Holly Golightly. They would never change because they'd been given their character too soon; which, like sudden riches, leads to a lack of proportion: the one had splurged herself into a top-heavy realist, the other a lopsided romantic. I imagined them in a restaurant of the future, Mildred still studying the menu for its nutritional values, Holly still gluttonous for everything on it. It would never be different. They would walk through life and out of it with the same determined step that took small notice of those cliffs at the left. Such profound observations made me forget where I was; I came to, startled to find myself in the gloom of the library, and surprised all over again to see Holly there. It was after seven, she was freshening her lipstick and perking up her appearance from what she deemed correct for a library to what, by adding a bit of scarf, some earrings, she considered suitable for the Colony. When she'd left, I wandered over to the table where her books remained; they were what I had wanted to see. *South by Thunderbird. Byways of Brazil. The Political Mind of Latin America.* And so forth.

On Christmas Eve she and Mag gave a party. Holly asked me to come early and help trim the tree, I'm still not sure how they maneuvered that tree into the apartment. The top branches were crushed against the ceiling, the lower ones spread wall-to-wall; altogether it was not unlike the yuletide giant we see in Rockefeller Plaza. Moreover, it would have taken a Rockefeller to decorate it, for it soaked up baubles and tinsel like melting snow. Holly suggested she run out to Woolworth's and steal some balloons; she did: and they turned the tree into a fairly good show. We made a toast to our work, and Holly said: "Look in the bedroom. There's a present for you."

I had one for her, too: a small package in my pocket that felt even smaller when I saw, square on the bed and wrapped with a red ribbon, the beautiful bird cage.

"But, Holly! It's dreadful!"

"I couldn't agree more; but I thought you wanted it."

"The money! Three hundred and fifty dollars!"

She shrugged. "A few extra trips to the powder room. Promise me, though. Promise you'll never put a living thing in it."

I started to kiss her, but she held out her hand. "Gimme," she said, tapping the bulge in my pocket.

"I'm afraid it isn't much," and it wasn't: a St. Christopher's medal. But at least it came from Tiffany's.

HOLLY WAS NOT A GIRL who could keep anything, and surely by now she has lost that medal, left it in a suitcase or some hotel drawer. But the bird cage is still mine. I've lugged it to New Orleans, Nantucket, all over Europe, Morocco, the West Indies. Yet I seldom remember that it was Holly who gave it to me, because at one point I chose to forget: we had a big falling-out, and among the objects rotating in the eye of our hurricane were the bird cage and O.J. Berman and my story, a copy of which I'd given Holly when it appeared in the university review.

Sometime in February, Holly had gone on a winter trip with Rusty, Mag and José Ybarra-Jaegar. Our altercation happened soon after she returned. She was brown as iodine, her hair was sun-bleached to a ghost-color, she'd had a wonderful time: "Well, first of all we were in Key West, and Rusty got mad at some sailors, or vice versa, *any*way he'll have to wear a spine brace the rest of his life. Dearest Mag ended up in the hospital, too. First-degree sunburn. Disgusting: all blisters and citronella. We couldn't stand the smell of her. So José and I left them in the hospital and went to Havana. He says wait till I see Rio; but as far as I'm concerned Havana can take my money right now. We had an irresistible guide, most of him Negro and the rest of him Chinese, and while I don't go much for one or the other, the combination was fairly riveting: so I let him play kneesie under the table, because frankly I didn't find him at all banal; but then one night he took us to a blue movie, and what do you suppose? There *he* was *on* the screen. Of course when we got back to Key West, Mag was positive

I'd spent the whole time sleeping with José. So was Rusty: but he doesn't care about that, he simply wants to hear the details. Actually, things were pretty tense until I had a heart-to-heart with Mag."

We were in the front room, where, though it was now nearly March, the enormous Christmas tree, turned brown and scentless, its balloons shriveled as an old cow's dugs, still occupied most of the space. A recognizable piece of furniture had been added to the room: an army cot; and Holly, trying to preserve her tropic look, was sprawled on it under a sun lamp.

"And you convinced her?"

"That I hadn't slept with José? God, yes. I simply told—but you know: made it sound like an *ag*onized confession—simply told her I was a dyke."

"She couldn't have believed that."

"The hell she didn't. Why do you think she went out and bought this army cot? Leave it to me: I'm always top banana in the shock department. Be a darling, darling, rub some oil on my back." While I was performing this service, she said: "O.J. Berman's in town, and listen, I gave him your story in the magazine. He was quite impressed. He thinks maybe you're worth helping. But he says you're on the wrong track. Negroes and children: who cares?"

"Not Mr. Berman, I gather."

"Well, I agree with him. I read that story twice. Brats and niggers. Trembling leaves. *Description.* It doesn't *mean* anything."

My hand, smoothing oil on her skin, seemed to have a temper of its own: it yearned to raise itself and come down on her buttocks. "Give me an example," I said quietly. "Of something that means something. In your opinion."

"*Wuthering Heights,*" she said, without hesitation.

The urge in my hand was growing beyond control. "But that's unreasonable. You're talking about a work of genius."

"It was, wasn't it? *My wild sweet Cathy.* God, I cried buckets. I saw it ten times."

I said, "Oh" with recognizable relief, "oh" with a shameful, rising inflection, "the *movie.*"

Her muscles hardened, the touch of her was like stone warmed by the sun. "Everybody has to feel superior to somebody," she said. "But it's customary to present a little proof before you take the privilege."

"I don't compare myself to you. Or Berman. Therefore I can't feel superior. We want different things."

"Don't you want to make money?"

"I haven't planned that far."

"That's how your stories sound. As though you'd written them without knowing the end. Well, I'll tell you: you'd better make money. You have an expensive imagination. Not many people are going to buy you bird cages."

"Sorry."

"You will be if you hit me. You wanted to a minute ago: I could feel it in your hand; and you want to now."

I did, terribly; my hand, my heart was shaking as I recapped the bottle of oil. "Oh no, I wouldn't regret that. I'm only sorry you wasted your money on me: Rusty Trawler is too hard a way of earning it."

She sat up on the army cot, her face, her naked breasts coldly blue in the sun-lamp light. "It should take you about four seconds to walk from here to the door. I'll give you two."

I WENT STRAIGHT UPSTAIRS, GOT the bird cage, took it down and left it in front of her door. That settled that. Or so I imagined until the next morning when, as I was leaving for work, I saw the cage perched on a sidewalk ashcan waiting for the garbage collector. Rather sheepishly, I rescued it and carried it back to my room, a capitulation that did not lessen my resolve to put Holly Golightly absolutely out of my life. She was, I decided, "a crude exhibitionist," "a time waster," "an utter fake": someone never to be spoken to again.

And I didn't. Not for a long while. We passed each other on the stairs with lowered eyes. If she walked into Joe Bell's, I walked out. At one point, Madame Sapphia Spanella, the coloratura and roller-skating enthusiast who lived on the first floor, circulated a petition among the brownstone's other tenants asking them to join her in having Miss Golightly evicted: she was, said Madame Spanella, "morally objectionable" and the "perpetrator of all-night gatherings that endanger the safety and sanity of her neighbors." Though I refused to sign, secretly I felt Madame Spanella had cause to complain. But her petition failed, and as April approached May, the open-windowed, warm spring nights were lurid with the party sounds, the loud-playing phonograph and martini laughter that emanated from Apt. 2.

It was no novelty to encounter suspicious specimens among Holly's callers, quite the contrary; but one day late that spring, while passing through the brownstone's vestibule, I noticed a *very* provocative man examining her mailbox. A person in his early fifties with a hard, weathered face, gray forlorn eyes. He wore an old sweat-stained gray hat, and his cheap summer suit, a pale blue, hung too loosely on his lanky frame; his shoes were brown and brand-new. He seemed to have no intention of ringing Holly's bell. Slowly, as though he were reading Braille, he kept rubbing a finger across the embossed lettering of her name.

That evening, on my way to supper, I saw the man again. He was standing across the street, leaning against a tree and staring up at Holly's windows. Sinister speculations rushed through my head. Was he a detective? Or some underworld agent connected with her Sing Sing friend, Sally Tomato? The situation revived my tenderer feelings for Holly; it was only fair to interrupt our feud long enough to warn her that she was being watched. As I walked to the corner, heading east toward the Hamburg Heaven at Seventy-ninth and Madison, I could feel the man's attention focused on me. Presently, without turning my head, I knew that he was following me. Because I could hear him whistling. Not any ordinary tune, but the plaintive, prairie melody Holly sometimes played on her guitar: *Don't wanna sleep, don't wanna die, just wanna go a-travelin' through the pastures of the sky.* The whistling continued across Park Avenue and up Madison. Once, while waiting for a traffic light to change, I watched him out of the corner of my eye as he stooped to pet a sleazy Pomeranian. "That's a fine animal you got there," he told the owner in a hoarse, countrified drawl.

Hamburg Heaven was empty. Nevertheless, he took a seat right beside me at the long counter. He smelled of tobacco and sweat. He ordered a cup of coffee, but when it came he didn't touch it. Instead, he chewed on a toothpick and studied me in the wall mirror facing us.

"Excuse me," I said, speaking to him via the mirror, "but what do you want?"

The question didn't embarrass him; he seemed relieved to have had it asked. "Son," he said, "I need a friend."

He brought out a wallet. It was as worn as his leathery hands, almost falling to pieces; and so was the brittle, cracked, blurred snapshot he handed me. There were seven people in the picture, all grouped together on the sagging porch of a stark wooden house, and all children, except for the man himself, who had his arm around the waist of a plump blond little girl with a hand shading her eyes against the sun.

"That's me," he said, pointing at himself. "That's her . . ." he tapped the plump girl. "And this one over here," he added, indicating a tow-headed beanpole, "that's her brother, Fred."

I looked at "her" again: and yes, now I could see it, an embryonic resemblance to Holly in the squinting, fat-cheeked child. At the same moment, I realized who the man must be.

"You're Holly's *father.*"

He blinked, he frowned. "Her name's not Holly. She was a Lulamae Barnes. Was," he said, shifting the toothpick in his mouth, "till she married me. I'm her husband. Doc Golightly. I'm a horse doctor, animal man. Do some farming, too. Near Tulip, Texas. Son, why are you laughin'?"

It wasn't real laughter: it was nerves. I took a swallow of water and choked; he pounded me on the back. "This here's no humorous matter, son. I'm a tired man. I've been five years lookin' for my woman. Soon as I got that letter from Fred, saying where she was, I bought myself a ticket on the Greyhound. Lulamae belongs home with her husband and her churren."

"Children?"

"*Them's* her churren," he said, almost shouted. He meant the four other young faces in the picture, two barefooted girls and a pair of overalled boys. Well, of course: the man was deranged. "But Holly can't be the mother of those children. They're older than she is. Bigger."

"Now, son," he said in a reasoning voice, "I didn't claim they was her natural-born churren. Their own precious mother, precious woman, Jesus rest her soul, she passed away July 4th, Independence Day, 1936. The year of the drought. When I married Lulamae, that was in December, 1938, she was going on fourteen. Maybe an ordinary person, being only fourteen, wouldn't know their right mind. But you take Lulamae, she was an exceptional woman. She knew good-and-well what she was doing when she promised to be my wife and the mother of my churren. She plain broke our hearts when she ran off like she done." He sipped his cold coffee, and glanced at me with a searching earnestness. "Now, son, do you doubt me? Do you believe what I'm saying is so?"

I did. It was too implausible not to be fact; moreover, it dovetailed with O.J. Berman's description of the Holly he'd first encountered in California: "You don't know whether she's a hillbilly or an Okie or what." Berman couldn't be blamed for not guessing that she was a child-wife from Tulip, Texas.

"Plain broke our hearts when she ran off like she done," the horse doctor repeated. "She had no cause. All the housework was done by her daughters. Lulamae could just take it easy: fuss in front of mirrors and wash her hair. Our own cows, our own garden, chickens, pigs: son, that woman got positively fat. While her brother growed into a giant. Which is a sight different from how they come to us. 'Twas Nellie, my oldest girl, 'twas Nellie brought 'em into the house. She come to me one morning, and said: 'Papa, I got two wild yunguns locked in the kitchen. I caught 'em outside stealing milk and turkey eggs.' That was Lulamae and Fred. Well, you never saw a more pitiful something. Ribs sticking out everywhere, legs so puny they can't hardly stand, teeth wobbling so bad they can't chew mush. Story was: their mother died of the TB, and their papa done the same—and all the churren, a whole raft of 'em, they been sent off to live with different mean people. Now Lulamae and her brother, them two been living with some mean, no-count people a hundred miles east of Tulip. She had good cause to run off from that house. She didn't have none to leave mine. 'Twas her home." He leaned his elbows on the counter and, pressing his closed eyes with his fingertips, sighed. "She plumped out to be a real pretty woman. Lively, too. Talky as a jaybird. With something smart to say on every subject: better than the radio. First thing you know, I'm out picking flowers. I tamed her a crow and taught it to say her name. I showed her how to play the guitar. Just to look at her made the tears spring to my eyes. The night I proposed, I cried like a baby. She said: 'What you want to cry for, Doc? 'Course we'll be married. I've never been married before.' Well, I had to laugh, hug and squeeze her: *never been married before!*" He chuckled, chewed on his toothpick a moment. "Don't tell me that woman wasn't happy!" he said, challengingly. "We all doted on her. She didn't have to lift a finger, 'cept to eat a piece of pie. 'Cept to comb her hair and send away for all the magazines. We must've had a hunnerd dollars' worth of magazines come into that house. Ask me, that's what done it. Looking at show-off pictures. Reading dreams. That's what started her walking down the road. Every day she'd walk a little further: a mile, and come home. Two miles, and come home. One day she just kept on." He put his hands over his eyes again; his breathing made a ragged noise. "The crow I give her went wild and flew away. All summer you could hear him. In the yard. In the garden. In the woods. All summer that damned bird was calling: Lulamae, Lulamae."

He stayed hunched over and silent, as though listening to the long-ago summer sound. I carried our checks to the cashier. While I was paying, he joined me. We left together and walked over to Park Avenue. It was a cool, blowy evening; swanky awnings flapped in the breeze. The quietness between us continued until I said: "But what about her brother? He didn't leave?"

"No, sir," he said, clearing his throat. "Fred was with us right till they took him in the Army. A fine boy. Fine with horses. He didn't know what got into Lulamae, how come she left her brother and husband and churren. After he was in the Army, though, Fred started hearing from her. The other day he wrote me her address. So I come to get her. I know she's sorry for what she done. I know she wants to go home." He seemed to be asking me to agree with him. I told him that I thought he'd find Holly, or Lulamae, somewhat changed. "Listen, son," he said, as we reached the steps of the brownstone, "I advised you I need a friend. Because I don't want to surprise her. Scare her none. That's why I've held off. Be my friend: let her know I'm here."

The notion of introducing Mrs. Golightly to her husband had its satisfying aspects; and, glancing up at her lighted windows, I hoped her friends were there, for the prospect of watching the Texan shake hands with Mag and Rusty and José was more satisfying still. But Doc Golightly's proud earnest eyes and sweat-stained hat made me ashamed of such anticipations. He followed me into the house and prepared to wait at the bottom of the stairs. "Do I look nice?" he whispered, brushing his sleeves, tightening the knot of his tie.

Holly was alone. She answered the door at once; in fact, she was on her way out—white satin dancing pumps and quantities of perfume announced gala intentions. "Well, idiot," she said, and playfully slapped me with her purse. "I'm in too much of a hurry to make up now. We'll smoke the pipe tomorrow, okay?"

"Sure, Lulamae. If you're still around tomorrow."

She took off her dark glasses and squinted at me. It was as though her eyes were shattered prisms, the dots of blue and gray and green like broken bits of sparkle. "*He* told you that," she said in a small, shivering voice. "Oh, please. *Where* is he?" She ran past me into the hall. "Fred!" she called down the stairs. "Fred! Where are you, darling?"

I could hear Doc Golightly's footsteps climbing the stairs. His head appeared above the banisters, and Holly backed away from him, not as though she were frightened, but as though she were retreating into a shell of disappointment. Then he was standing in front of her, hangdog and shy. "Gosh, Lulamae," he began, and hesitated, for Holly was gazing at him vacantly, as though she couldn't place him. "Gee, honey," he said, "don't they feed you up here? You're so skinny. Like when I first saw you. All wild around the eye."

Holly touched his face; her fingers tested the reality of his chin, his beard stubble. "Hello, Doc," she said gently, and kissed him on the cheek. "Hello, Doc," she repeated happily, as he lifted her off her feet in a rib-crushing grip. Whoops of relieved laughter shook him. "Gosh, Lulamae. Kingdom come."

Neither of them noticed me when I squeezed past them and went up to my room. Nor did they seem aware of Madame Sapphia Spanella, who opened her door and yelled: "Shut up! It's a disgrace. Do your whoring elsewhere."

"*DIVORCE* HIM? OF COURSE I never divorced him. I was only fourteen, for God's sake. It couldn't have been *legal*." Holly tapped an empty martini glass. "Two more, my darling Mr. Bell."

Joe Bell, in whose bar we were sitting, accepted the order reluctantly. "You're rockin' the boat kinda early," he complained, crunching on a Tums. It was not yet noon, according to the black mahogany clock behind the bar, and he'd already served us three rounds.

"But it's Sunday, Mr. Bell. Clocks are slow on Sundays. Besides, I haven't been to bed yet," she told him, and confided to me: "Not to sleep." She blushed, and glanced away guiltily. For the first time since I'd known her, she seemed to feel a need to justify herself: "Well, I had to. Doc really loves me, you know. And I love him. He may have looked old and tacky to *you*. But you don't know the sweetness of him, the confidence he can give to birds and brats and fragile things like that. Anyone who ever gave you confidence, you owe them a lot. I've always remembered Doc in my prayers. Please stop smirking!" she demanded, stabbing out a cigarette. "I *do* say my prayers."

"I'm not smirking. I'm smiling. You're the most amazing person."

"I suppose I am," she said, and her face, wan, rather bruised-looking in the morning light, brightened; she smoothed her tousled hair, and the colors of it glimmered like a shampoo advertisement. "I must look fierce. But who wouldn't? We spent the rest of the night roaming around in a bus station. Right up till the last minute Doc thought I was going to go with him. Even though I kept telling him: But, Doc, I'm not fourteen any more, and I'm not Lulamae. But the terrible part is (and I realized it while we were standing there) I am. I'm still stealing turkey eggs and running through a brier patch. Only now I call it having the mean reds."

Joe Bell disdainfully settled the fresh martinis in front of us.

"Never love a wild thing, Mr. Bell," Holly advised him. "That was Doc's mistake. He was always lugging home wild things. A hawk with a hurt wing. One time it was a full-grown bobcat with a broken leg. But you can't give your heart to a wild thing: the more you do, the stronger they get. Until they're strong enough to run into the woods. Or fly into a tree. Then a taller tree. Then the sky. That's how you'll end up, Mr. Bell. If you let yourself love a wild thing. You'll end up looking at the sky."

"She's drunk," Joe Bell informed me.

"Moderately," Holly confessed. "But Doc knew what I meant. I explained it to him very carefully, and it was something he could understand. We shook hands and held on to each other and he wished me luck." She glanced at the clock. "He must be in the Blue Mountains by now."

"What's she talkin' about?" Joe Bell asked me.

Holly lifted her martini. "Let's wish the Doc luck, too," she said, touching her glass against mine. "Good luck: and believe me, dearest Doc—it's better to look at the sky than live there. Such an empty place; so vague. Just a country where the thunder goes and things disappear."

TRAWLER MARRIES FOURTH. I WAS on a subway somewhere in Brooklyn when I saw that headline. The paper that bannered it belonged to another passenger. The only part of the text that I could see read: *Rutherfurd "Rusty" Trawler, the millionaire playboy often accused of pro-Nazi sympathies, eloped to Greenwich yesterday with a beautiful*—Not that I wanted to read any more. Holly had married him: well, well. I wished I were under the wheels of the train. But I'd been wishing that before I spotted the headline. For a headful of reasons. I hadn't seen Holly, not really, since our drunken Sunday at Joe Bell's bar. The intervening weeks had given me my own case of the mean reds. First off, I'd been fired from my job: deservedly, and for an amusing misdemeanor too complicated to recount here. Also, my draft board was displaying an uncomfortable interest; and, having so recently escaped the regimentation of a small town, the idea of entering another form of disciplined life made me desperate. Between the uncertainty of my draft status and a lack of specific experience, I couldn't seem to find another job. That was what I was doing on a subway in Brooklyn: returning from a discouraging interview with an editor of the now defunct newspaper, *PM*. All this, combined with the city heat of the summer, had reduced me to a state of nervous inertia. So I more than half meant it when I wished I were under the wheels of the train. The headline made the desire quite positive. If Holly could marry that "absurd foetus," then the army of wrongness rampant in the world might as well march over me. Or, and the question is apparent, was my outrage a little the result of being in love with Holly myself? A little. For I *was* in love with her. Just as I'd once been in love with my mother's elderly colored cook and a postman who let me follow him on his rounds and a whole family named McKendrick. That category of love generates jealousy, too.

When I reached my station I bought a paper; and, reading the tail-end of that sentence, discovered that Rusty's bride was: *a beautiful cover girl from the Arkansas hills, Miss Margaret Thatcher Fitzhue Wildwood.* Mag! My legs went so limp with relief I took a taxi the rest of the way home.

Madame Sapphia Spanella met me in the hall, wild-eyed and wringing her hands. "Run," she said. "Bring the police. She is killing somebody! Somebody is killing her!"

It sounded like it. As though tigers were loose in Holly's

apartment. A riot of crashing glass, of rippings and fallings and overturned furniture. But there were no quarreling voices inside the uproar, which made it seem unnatural. "Run," shrieked Madame Spanella, pushing me. "Tell the police murder!"

I ran; but only upstairs to Holly's door. Pounding on it had one result: the racket subsided. Stopped altogether. But pleadings to let me in went unanswered, and my efforts to break down the door merely culminated in a bruised shoulder. Then below I heard Madame Spanella commanding some newcomer to go for the police. "Shut up," she was told, "and get out of my way."

It was José Ybarra-Jaegar. Looking not at all the smart Brazilian diplomat; but sweaty and frightened. He ordered me out of his way, too. And, using his own key, opened the door. "In here, Dr. Goldman," he said, beckoning to a man accompanying him.

Since no one prevented me, I followed them into the apartment, which was tremendously wrecked. At last the Christmas tree had been dismantled, very literally: its brown dry branches sprawled in a welter of torn-up books, broken lamps and phonograph records. Even the icebox had been emptied, its contents tossed around the room: raw eggs were sliding down the walls, and in the midst of the debris Holly's no-name cat was calmly licking a puddle of milk.

In the bedroom, the smell of smashed perfume bottles made me gag. I stepped on Holly's dark glasses; they were lying on the floor, the lenses already shattered, the frames cracked in half.

Perhaps that is why Holly, a rigid figure on the bed, stared at José so blindly, seemed not to see the doctor, who, testing her pulse, crooned: "You're a tired young lady. Very tired. You want to go to sleep, don't you? Sleep."

Holly rubbed her forehead, leaving a smear of blood from a cut finger. "Sleep," she said, and whimpered like an exhausted, fretful child. "He's the only one would ever let me. Let me hug him on cold nights. I saw a place in Mexico. With horses. By the sea."

"With horses by the sea," lullabied the doctor, selecting from his black case a hypodermic.

José averted his face, queasy at the sight of a needle. "Her sickness is only grief?" he asked, his difficult English lending the question an unintended irony. "She is grieving only?"

"Didn't hurt a bit, now did it?" inquired the doctor, smugly dabbing Holly's arm with a scrap of cotton.

She came to sufficiently to focus the doctor. "*Everything* hurts. Where are my glasses?" But she didn't need them. Her eyes were closing of their own accord.

"She is only grieving?" insisted José.

"Please, sir," the doctor was quite short with him, "if you will leave me alone with the patient."

José withdrew to the front room, where he released his temper on the snooping, tiptoeing presence of Madame Spanella. "Don't touch me! I'll call the police," she threatened as he whipped her to the door with Portuguese oaths.

He considered throwing me out, too; or so I surmised from his expression. Instead, he invited me to have a drink. The only unbroken bottle we could find contained dry vermouth. "I have a worry," he confided. "I have a worry that this should cause scandal. Her crashing everything. Conducting like a crazy. I must have no public scandal. It is too delicate: my name, my work."

He seemed cheered to learn that I saw no reason for a "scandal"; demolishing one's own possessions was, presumably, a private affair.

"It is only a question of grieving," he firmly declared.

"When the sadness came, first she throws the drink she is drinking. The bottle. Those books. A lamp. Then I am scared. I hurry to bring a doctor."

"But why?" I wanted to know. "Why should she have a fit over Rusty? If I were her, I'd celebrate."

"Rusty?"

I was still carrying my newspaper, and showed him the headline.

"Oh, that." He grinned rather scornfully. "They do us a grand favor, Rusty and Mag. We laugh over it: how they think they break our hearts when all the time we *want* them to run away. I assure you, we were laughing when the sadness came." His eyes searched the litter on the floor; he picked up a ball of yellow paper. "This," he said.

It was a telegram from Tulip, Texas: *Received notice young Fred killed in action overseas stop your husband and children join in the sorrow of our mutual loss stop letter follows love Doc.*

HOLLY NEVER MENTIONED HER BROTHER again: except once. Moreover, she stopped calling me Fred. June, July, all through the warm months she hibernated like a winter animal who did not know spring had come and gone. Her hair darkened, she put on weight. She became rather careless about her clothes: used to rush round to the delicatessen wearing a rain-slicker and nothing underneath. José moved into the apartment, his name replacing Mag Wildwood's on the mailbox. Still, Holly was a good deal alone, for José stayed in Washington three days a week. During his absences she entertained no one and seldom left the apartment—except on Thursdays, when she made her weekly trip to Ossining.

Which is not to imply that she had lost interest in life; far from it, she seemed more content, altogether happier than I'd ever seen her. A keen sudden un-Holly-like enthusiasm for homemaking resulted in several un-Holly-like purchases: at a Parke-Bernet auction she acquired a stag-at-bay hunting tapestry and, from the William Randolph Hearst estate, a gloomy pair of Gothic "easy" chairs; she bought the complete Modern Library, shelves of classical records, innumerable Metropolitan Museum reproductions (including a statue of a Chinese cat that her own cat hated and hissed at and ultimately broke), a Waring mixer and a pressure cooker and a library of cook books. She spent whole hausfrau afternoons slopping about in the sweatbox of her midget kitchen: "José says I'm better than the Colony. Really, who would have dreamed I had such a great natural talent? A month ago I couldn't scramble eggs." And still couldn't, for that matter. Simple dishes, steak, a proper salad, were beyond her. Instead, she fed José, and occasionally myself, *outré* soups (brandied black terrapin poured into avocado shells) Nero-ish novelties (roasted pheasant stuffed with pomegranates and persimmons) and other dubious innovations (chicken and saffron rice served with a chocolate sauce: "An East Indian classic, *my* dear.") Wartime sugar and cream rationing restricted her imagination when it came to sweets—nevertheless, she once managed something called Tobacco Tapioca: best not describe it.

Nor describe her attempts to master Portuguese, an ordeal as tedious to me as it was to her, for whenever I visited her an album of Linguaphone records never ceased rotating on the phonograph. Now, too, she rarely spoke a sentence that did not begin, "After we're married—" or "When we move to Rio—" Yet José had never suggested marriage. She admitted it. "But, after all, he *knows* I'm preggers. Well, I am, darling. Six weeks gone. I don't see why *that* should surprise you. It didn't me. Not *un peu* bit. I'm delighted. I want to have at least nine. I'm sure some of them will be rather dark—José has a touch of *le nègre,* I suppose you guessed that? Which is fine by me: what could be prettier than a quite coony baby with bright green beautiful eyes? I wish, please don't laugh—but I wish I'd been a virgin for him, for José. Not that I've warmed the multitudes some people say: I don't blame the bastards for *saying* it, I've always thrown out such a jazzy line. Really, though, I toted up the other night, and I've only had eleven lovers—not counting anything that happened before I was thirteen because, after all, that just *doesn't* count. Eleven. Does that make me a whore? Look at Mag Wildwood. Or Honey Tucker. Or Rose Ellen Ward. They've had the old clap-yo'-hands so many times it amounts to applause. Of course I haven't anything *against* whores. Except this: some of them may have an honest tongue but they all have dishonest hearts. I mean, you can't bang the guy and cash his checks and at least not *try* to believe you love him. I never have. Even Benny Shacklett and all those rodents. I sort of hypnotized myself into thinking their sheer rattiness had a certain allure. Actually, except for Doc, if you want to count Doc, José is my first non-rat romance. Oh, he's not my idea of the absolute finito. He tells little lies and he worries what people *think* and he takes about fifty baths a day: men ought to smell *some*what. He's too prim, too cautious to be my guy ideal; he always turns his back to get undressed and he makes too much noise when he eats and I don't like to see him run because there's something funny-looking about him when he runs. If I were free to choose from everybody alive, just snap my fingers and say come here you, I wouldn't pick José. Nehru, he's nearer the mark. Wendell

Willkie. I'd settle for Garbo any day. Why not? A person ought to be able to marry men or women or—listen, if you came to me and said you wanted to hitch up with Man O' War, I'd respect your feeling. No, I'm serious. Love should be allowed. I'm all for it. Now that I've got a pretty good idea what it is. Because I *do* love José—I'd stop smoking if he asked me to. He's *friendly,* he can laugh me out of the mean reds, only I don't have them much any more, except sometimes, and even then they're not so hideola that I gulp Seconal or have to haul myself to Tiffany's: I take his suit to the cleaner, or stuff some mushrooms, and I feel fine, just great. Another thing, I've thrown away my horoscopes. I must have spent a dollar on every goddamn star in the goddamn planetarium. It's a bore, but the answer is good things only happen to you if you're good. Good? Honest is more what I mean. Not law-type honest—I'd rob a grave, I'd steal two-bits off a dead man's eyes if I thought it would contribute to the day's enjoyment—but unto-thyself-type honest. Be anything but a coward, a pretender, an emotional crook, a whore: I'd rather have cancer than a dishonest heart. Which isn't being pious. Just practical. Cancer *may* cool you, but the other's sure to. Oh, screw it, cookie—hand me my guitar and I'll sing you a *fado* in *the* most perfect Portuguese."

Those final weeks, spanning end of summer and the beginning of another autumn, are blurred in memory, perhaps because our understanding of each other had reached that sweet depth where two people communicate more often in silence than in words: an affectionate quietness replaces the tensions, the unrelaxed chatter and chasing about that produce a friendship's more showy, more, in the surface sense, dramatic moments. Frequently, when *he* was out of town (I'd developed hostile attitudes toward *him,* and seldom used his name) we spent entire evenings together during which we exchanged less than a hundred words; once, we walked all the way to Chinatown, ate a chow-mein supper, bought some paper lanterns and stole a box of joss sticks, then moseyed across the Brooklyn Bridge, and on the bridge, as we watched seaward-moving ships pass between the cliffs of burning skyline, she said: "Years from now, years and years, one of those ships will bring me back, me and my nine Brazilian brats. Because yes, they *must* see this, these lights, the river—I love New York, even though it isn't mine, the way something has to be, a tree or a street or a house, something, anyway, that belongs to me because I belong to it." And I said: "Do shut up," for I felt infuriatingly left out—a tugboat in dry-dock while she, glittery voyager of secure destination, steamed down the harbor with whistles whistling and confetti in the air.

So the days, the last days, blow about in memory, hazy, autumnal, all alike as leaves: until a day unlike any other I've lived.

IT HAPPENED TO FALL ON the 30th of September, my birthday, a fact which had no effect on events, except that, expecting some form of monetary remembrance from my family, I was eager for the postman's morning visit. Indeed, I went downstairs and waited for him. If I had not been loitering in the vestibule, then Holly would not have asked me to go horseback riding; and would not, consequently, have had the opportunity to save my life.

"Come on," she said, when she found me awaiting the postman. "Let's walk a couple of horses around the park." She was wearing a windbreaker and a pair of blue jeans and tennis shoes; she slapped her stomach, drawing attention to its flatness: "Don't think I'm out to lose the heir. But there's a horse, my darling old Mabel Minerva—I can't go without saying good-bye to Mabel Minerva."

"Good-bye?"

"A week from Saturday. José bought the tickets." In rather a trance, I let her lead me down to the street. "We change planes in Miami. Then over the sea. Over the Andes. Taxi!"

Over the Andes. As we rode in a cab across Central Park it seemed to me as though I, too, were flying, desolately floating over snow-peaked and perilous territory.

"But you can't. After all, what about. Well, what about. Well, you can't *really* run off and leave everybody."

"I don't think anyone will miss me. I have no friends."

"I will. Miss you. So will Joe Bell. And oh—millions. Like Sally. Poor Mr. Tomato."

"I loved old Sally," she said, and sighed. "You know I haven't been to see him in a month? When I told him I was going away, he was an angel. *Actually*"—she frowned—"he seemed *delighted* that I was leaving the country. He said it was all for the best. Because sooner or later there might be trouble. If they found out I wasn't his real niece. That fat lawyer, O'Shaughnessy, O'Shaughnessy sent me five hundred dollars. In cash. A wedding present from Sally."

I wanted to be unkind. "You can expect a present from me, too. When, and if, the wedding happens."

She laughed. "He'll marry me, all right. In church. And with his family there. That's why we're waiting till we get to Rio."

"Does he know you're married already?"

"What's the matter with you? Are you trying to ruin the day? It's a beautiful day: leave it alone!"

"But it's perfectly possible—"

"It *isn't* possible. I've told you, that wasn't legal. It *couldn't* be." She rubbed her nose, and glanced at me sideways. "Mention that to a living soul, darling. I'll hang you by your toes and dress you for a hog."

The stables—I believe they have been replaced by television studios—were on West Sixty-sixth street. Holly selected for me an old sway-back black and white mare: "Don't worry, she's safer than a cradle." Which, in my case, was a necessary guarantee, for ten-cent pony rides at childhood carnivals were the limit of my equestrian experience. Holly helped hoist me into the saddle, then mounted her own horse, a silvery animal that took the lead as we jogged across the traffic of Central Park West and entered a riding path dappled with leaves denuding breezes danced about.

"See?" she shouted. "It's great!"

And suddenly it was. Suddenly, watching the tangled colors of Holly's hair flash in the red-yellow leaf light, I loved her enough to forget myself, my self-pitying despairs, and be content that something she thought happy was going to happen. Very gently the horses began to trot, waves of wind splashed us, spanked our faces, we plunged in and out of sun and shadow pools, and joy, a glad-to-be-alive exhilaration, jolted through me like a jigger of nitrogen. That was one minute; the next introduced farce in grim disguise.

For all at once, like savage members of a jungle ambush, a band of Negro boys leapt out of the shrubbery along the path. Hooting, cursing, they launched rocks and thrashed at the horse's rumps with switches.

Mine, the black and white mare, rose on her hind legs, whinnied, teetered like a tightrope artist, then blue-streaked down the path, bouncing my feet out of the stirrups and leaving me scarcely attached. Her hooves made the gravel stones spit sparks. The sky careened. Trees, a lake with little-boy sailboats, statues went by licketysplit. Nursemaids rushed to rescue their charges from our awesome approach; men, bums and others, yelled: "Pull in the reins!" and "Whoa, boy, whoa!" and "Jump!" It was only later that I remembered these voices; at the time I was simply conscious of Holly, the cowboy-sound of her racing behind me, never quite catching up, and over and over calling encouragements. Onward: across the park and out into Fifth Avenue: stampeding against the noonday traffic, taxis, buses that screechingly swerved. Past the Duke mansion, the Frick Museum, past the Pierre and the Plaza. But Holly gained ground; moreover, a mounted policeman had joined the chase: flanking my runaway mare, one on either side, their horses performed a pincer movement that brought her to a steamy halt. It was then, at last, that I fell off her back. Fell off and picked myself up and stood there, not altogether certain where I was. A crowd gathered. The policeman huffed and wrote in a book: presently he was most sympathetic, grinned and said he would arrange for our horses to be returned to their stable.

Holly put us in a taxi. "Darling. How do you feel?"

"Fine."

"But you haven't *any* pulse," she said, feeling my wrist.

"Then I must be dead."

"No, idiot. This is serious. Look at me."

The trouble was, I couldn't see her; rather, I saw several Hollys, a trio of sweaty faces so white with concern that I was both touched and embarrassed. "Honestly. I don't feel anything. Except ashamed."

"Please. Are you sure? Tell me the truth. You might have been killed."

"But I wasn't. And thank you. For saving my life. You're wonderful. Unique. I love you."

"Damn fool." She kissed me on the cheek. Then there were four of her, and I fainted dead away.

THAT EVENING, PHOTOGRAPHS OF HOLLY were front-paged by the late edition of the *Journal-American* and by the early editions of both the *Daily News* and the *Daily Mirror*. The publicity had nothing to do with runaway horses. It concerned quite another matter, as the headlines revealed: PLAYGIRL ARRESTED IN NARCOTICS SCANDAL (*Journal-American*), ARREST DOPE-SMUGGLING ACTRESS (*Daily News*), DRUG RING EXPOSED, GLAMOUR GIRL HELD (*Daily Mirror*).

Of the lot, the *News* printed the most striking picture: Holly, entering police headquarters, wedged between two muscular detectives, one male, one female. In this squalid context even her clothes (she was still wearing her riding costume, windbreaker and blue jeans) suggested a gang-moll hooligan: an impression dark glasses, disarrayed coiffure and a Picayune cigarette dangling from sullen lips did not diminish. The caption read: *Twenty-year-old Holly Golightly, beautiful movie starlet and café society celebrity D.A. alleges to be key figure in international drug-smuggling racket linked to racketeer Salvatore "Sally" Tomato. Dets. Patrick Connor and Sheilah Fezzonetti (L. and R.) are shown escorting her into 67th St. Precinct. See story on Pg. 3.* The story, featuring a photograph of a man identified as Oliver "Father" O'Shaughnessy (shielding his face with a fedora), ran three full columns. Here, somewhat condensed, are the pertinent paragraphs: *Members of café society were stunned today by the arrest of gorgeous Holly Golightly, twenty-year-old Hollywood starlet and highly publicized girl-about-New York. At the same time,* 2 P.M., *police nabbed Oliver O'Shaughnessy, 52, of the Hotel Seabord, W. 49th St., as he exited from a Hamburg Heaven on Madison Ave. Both are alleged by District Attorney Frank L. Donovan to be important figures in an international drug ring dominated by the notorious Mafia-führer Salvatore "Sally" Tomato, currently in Sing Sing serving a five-year rap for political bribery. . . . O'Shaughnessy, a defrocked priest variously known in crimeland circles as "Father" and "The Padre," has a history of arrests dating back to 1934, when he served two years for operating a phony Rhode Island mental institution, The Monastery. Miss Golightly, who has no previous criminal record, was arrested in her luxurious apartment at a swank East Side address. . . . Although the D.A.'s office has issued no formal statement, responsible sources insist the blond and beautiful actress, not long ago the constant companion of multimillionaire Rutherfurd Trawler, has been acting as "liaison" between the imprisoned Tomato and his chief-lieutenant, O'Shaughnessy. . . . Posing as a relative of Tomato's, Miss Golightly is said to have paid weekly visits to Sing Sing, and on these occasions Tomato supplied her with verbally coded messages which she then transmitted to O'Shaughnessy. Via this link, Tomato, believed to have been born in Cefalu, Sicily, in 1874, was able to keep first-hand control of a world-wide narcotics syndicate with outposts in Mexico, Cuba, Sicily, Tangier, Tehran and Dakar. But the D.A.'s office refused to offer any detail on these allegations or even verify them. . . . Tipped off, a large number of reporters were on hand at the E. 67th St. Precinct station when the accused pair arrived for booking. O'Shaughnessy, a burly red-haired man, refused comment and kicked one cameraman in the groin. But Miss Golightly, a fragile eyeful, even though attired like a tomboy in slacks and leather jacket, appeared relatively unconcerned. "Don't ask me what the hell this is about," she told reporters. "Parce-que je ne sais pas, mes chères. (Because I do not know, my dears).*

Yes—I have visited Sally Tomato. I used to go to see him every week. What's wrong with that? He believes in God, and so do I." . . . Then, under the subheading ADMITS OWN DRUG ADDICTION: *Miss Golightly smiled when a reporter asked whether or not she herself is a narcotics user. "I've had a little go at marijuana. It's not half so destructive as brandy. Cheaper, too. Unfortunately, I prefer brandy. No, Mr. Tomato never mentioned drugs to me. It makes me furious, the way these wretched people keep persecuting him. He's a sensitive, a religious person. A darling old man."*

There is one especially gross error in this report: she was not arrested in her "luxurious apartment." It took place in my own bathroom. I was soaking away my horse-ride pains in a tub of scalding water laced with Epsom salts; Holly, an attentive nurse, was sitting on the edge of the tub waiting to rub me with Sloan's liniment and tuck me into bed. There was a knock at the front door. As the door was unlocked, Holly called Come in. In came Madame Sapphia Spanella, trailed by a pair of civilian-clothed detectives, one of them a lady with thick yellow braids roped round her head.

"*Here* she is: the wanted woman!" boomed Madame Spanella, invading the bathroom and leveling a finger, first at Holly's, then my nakedness. "Look. What a whore she is." The male detective seemed embarrassed: by Madame Spanella and by the situation; but a harsh enjoyment tensed the face of his companion—she plumped a hand on Holly's shoulder and, in a surprising baby-child voice, said: "Come along, sister. You're going places." Whereupon Holly coolly told her: "Get them cotton-pickin' hands off of me, you dreary, driveling old bull-dyke." Which rather enraged the lady: she slapped Holly damned hard. So hard, her head twisted on her neck, and the bottle of liniment, flung from her hand, smithereened on the tile floor—where

I, scampering out of the tub to enrich the fray, stepped on it and all but severed both big toes. Nude and bleeding a path of bloody footprints, I followed the action as far as the hall. "Don't forget," Holly managed to instruct me as the detectives propelled her down the stairs, "please feed the cat."

OF COURSE I BELIEVED MADAME Spanella to blame: she'd several times called the authorities to complain about Holly. It didn't occur to me the affair could have dire dimensions until that evening when Joe Bell showed up flourishing the newspapers. He was too agitated to speak sensibly; he caroused the room hitting his fists together while I read the accounts.

Then he said: "You think it's so? She was mixed up in this lousy business?"

"Well, yes."

He popped a Tums in his mouth and, glaring at me, chewed it as though he were crunching my bones. "Boy, that's rotten. And you meant to be her friend. What a bastard!"

"Just a minute. I didn't say she was involved *knowingly.* She wasn't. But there, she did do it. Carry messages and whatnot—"

He said: "Take it pretty calm, don't you? Jesus, she could get ten years. More." He yanked the papers away from me. "You know her friends. These rich fellows. Come down to the bar, we'll start phoning. Our girl's going to need fancier shysters than I can afford."

I was too sore and shaky to dress myself; Joe Bell had to help. Back at his bar he propped me in the telephone booth with a triple martini and a brandy tumbler full of coins.

But I couldn't think who to contact. José was in Washington, and I had no notion where to reach him there. Rusty Trawler? Not that bastard! Only: what other friends of hers did I know? Perhaps she'd been right when she'd said she had none, not really.

I put through a call to Crestview 5-6958 in Beverly Hills, the number long-distance information gave me for O.J. Berman. The person who answered said Mr. Berman was having a massage and couldn't be disturbed: sorry, try later. Joe Bell was incensed—told me I should have said it was a life and death matter; and he insisted on my trying Rusty. First, I spoke to Mr. Trawler's butler—Mr. and Mrs. Trawler, he announced, were at dinner and might he take a message? Joe Bell shouted into the receiver: "This is urgent, mister. Life and death." The outcome was that I found myself talking—listening, rather—to the former Mag Wildwood: "Are you starkers?" she demanded. "My husband and I will positively *sue* anyone who attempts to connect our names with that ro-ro-ro*vol*ting and de-de-de*gen*erate girl. I always *knew* she was a hop-hop-head with no more morals than a hound-bitch in heat. Prison is where she belongs. And my husband agrees one thousand percent. We will positively *sue* anyone who—" Hanging up, I remembered old Doc down in Tulip, Texas; but no, Holly wouldn't like it if I called him, she'd kill me good.

I rang California again; the circuits were busy, stayed busy, and by the time O.J. Berman was on the line I'd emptied so many martinis he had to tell me why I was phoning him: "About the kid, is it? I know already. I spoke already to Iggy Fitelstein. Iggy's the best shingle in New York. I said Iggy you take care of it, send me the bill, only keep my name anonymous, see. Well, I owe the kid something. Not that I owe her *any*thing, you want to come down to it. She's crazy.

A phony. But a *real* phony, you know? Anyway, they only got her in ten thousand bail. Don't worry, Iggy'll spring her tonight—it wouldn't surprise me she's home already."

BUT SHE WASN'T; NOR HAD she returned the next morning when I went down to feed her cat. Having no key to the apartment, I used the fire escape and gained entrance through a window. The cat was in the bedroom, and he was not alone: a man was there, crouching over a suitcase. The two of us, each thinking the other a burglar, exchanged uncomfortable stares as I stepped through the window. He had a pretty face, lacquered hair, he resembled José; moreover, the suitcase he'd been packing contained the wardrobe José kept at Holly's, the shoes and suits she fussed over, was always carting to menders and cleaners. And I said, certain it was so: "Did Mr. Ybarra-Jaegar send you?"

"I am the cousin," he said with a wary grin and just-penetrable accent.

"Where is José?"

He repeated the question, as though translating it into another language. "Ah, *where* she is! She is waiting," he said and, seeming to dismiss me, resumed his valet activities.

So: the diplomat was planning a powder. Well, I wasn't amazed; or in the slightest sorry. Still, what a heartbreaking stunt: "He ought to be horsewhipped."

The cousin giggled, I'm sure he understood me. He shut the suitcase and produced a letter. "My cousin, she ask me leave that for his chum. You will oblige?"

On the envelope was scribbled: *For Miss H. Golightly—Courtesy Bearer.*

I sat down on Holly's bed, and hugged Holly's cat to me,

and felt as badly for Holly, every iota, as she could feel for herself.

"Yes, I will oblige."

AND I DID: WITHOUT THE least wanting to. But I hadn't the courage to destroy the letter; or the will power to keep it in my pocket when Holly very tentatively inquired if, if by any chance, I'd had news of José. It was two mornings later; I was sitting by her bedside in a room that reeked of iodine and bedpans, a hospital room. She had been there since the night of her arrest. "Well, darling," she'd greeted me, as I tiptoed toward her carrying a carton of Picayune cigarettes and a wheel of new-autumn violets, "I lost the heir." She looked not quite twelve years: her pale vanilla hair brushed back, her eyes, for once minus their dark glasses, clear as rain water—one couldn't believe how ill she'd been.

Yet it was true: "Christ, I nearly cooled. No fooling, the fat woman almost had me. She was yakking up a storm. I guess I couldn't have told you about the fat woman. Since I didn't know about her myself until my brother died. Right away I was wondering where he'd gone, what it meant, Fred's dying; and then I saw her, she was there in the room with me, and she had Fred cradled in her arms, a fat mean red bitch rocking in a rocking chair with Fred on her lap and laughing like a brass band. The mockery of it! But it's all that's ahead for us, my friend: this comedienne waiting to give you the old razz. Now do you see why I went crazy and broke everything?"

Except for the lawyer O.J. Berman had hired, I was the only visitor she had been allowed. Her room was shared by other patients, a trio of triplet-like ladies who, examining me with an interest not unkind but total, speculated in whispered Italian. Holly explained that: "They think you're my downfall, darling. The fellow what done me wrong"; and, to a suggestion that she set them straight, replied: "I can't. They don't speak English. Anyway, I wouldn't dream of spoiling their fun." It was then that she asked about José.

The instant she saw the letter she squinted her eyes and bent her lips in a tough tiny smile that advanced her age immeasurably. "Darling," she instructed me, "would you reach in the drawer there and give me my purse. A girl doesn't read this sort of thing without her lipstick."

Guided by a compact mirror, she powdered, painted every vestige of twelve-year-old out of her face. She shaped her lips with one tube, colored her cheeks from another. She penciled the rims of her eyes, blued the lids, sprinkled her neck with 4711; attached pearls to her ears and donned her dark glasses; thus armored, and after a displeased appraisal of her manicure's shabby condition, she ripped open the letter and let her eyes race through it while her stony small smile grew smaller and harder. Eventually she asked for a Picayune. Took a puff: "Tastes bum. But divine," she said and, tossing me the letter: "Maybe this will come in handy—if you ever write a rat-romance. Don't be hoggy: read it aloud. I'd like to hear it myself."

It began: "My dearest little girl—"

Holly at once interrupted. She wanted to know what I thought of the handwriting. I thought nothing: a tight, highly legible, uneccentric script. "It's him to a T. Buttoned up and constipated," she declared. "Go on."

"My dearest little girl, I have loved you knowing you were not as others. But conceive of my despair upon discovering in such a brutal and public style how very different you are from the manner of woman a man of my faith and career could hope to make his wife. Verily I grief for the disgrace of your present circumstance, and do not find it in my heart to add my condemn to the condemn that surrounds you. So I hope you will find it in your heart not to condemn me. I have my family to protect, and my name, and I am a coward where those institutions enter. Forget me, beautiful child. I am no longer here. I am gone home. But may God always be with you and your child. May God be not the same as—José."

"Well?"

"In a way it seems quite honest. And even touching."

"*Touching?* That square-ball jazz!"

"But after all, he *says* he's a coward; and from his point of view, you must see—"

Holly, however, did not want to admit that she saw; yet her face, despite its cosmetic disguise, confessed it. "All right, he's not a rat without reason. A super-sized, King Kong-type rat like Rusty. Benny Shacklett. But oh gee, golly goddamn," she said, jamming a fist into her mouth like a bawling baby, "I *did* love him. The rat."

The Italian trio imagined a lover's *crise* and, placing the blame for Holly's groanings where they felt it belonged, tut-tutted their tongues at me. I was flattered: proud that anyone should think Holly cared for me. She quieted when I offered her another cigarette. She swallowed and said: "Bless you, Buster. And bless you for being such a bad jockey. If I hadn't had to play Calamity Jane I'd still be looking forward to the grub in an unwed mama's home. Strenuous exercise, that's what did the trick. But I've scared *la merde* out of the whole badge-department by saying it was because Miss Dykeroo slapped me. Yessir, I can sue them on several counts, including false arrest."

Until then, we'd skirted mention of her more sinister

tribulations, and this jesting reference to them seemed appalling, pathetic, so definitely did it reveal how incapable she was of recognizing the bleak realities before her. "Now, Holly," I said, thinking: be strong, mature, an uncle. "Now, Holly. We can't treat it as a joke. We have to make plans."

"You're too young to be stuffy. Too small. By the way, what business is it of yours?"

"None. Except you're my friend, and I'm worried. I mean to know what you intend doing."

She rubbed her nose, and concentrated on the ceiling. "Today's Wednesday, isn't it? So I suppose I'll sleep until Saturday, really get a good *schluffen.* Saturday morning I'll skip out to the bank. Then I'll stop by the apartment and pick up a nightgown or two and my Mainbocher. Following which, I'll report to Idlewild. Where, as you damn well know, I have a perfectly fine reservation on a perfectly fine plane. And since you're such a friend I'll let you wave me off. *Please* stop shaking your head."

"Holly. Holly. You can't do that."

"*Et pourquoi pas?* I'm not hot-footing after José, if that's what you suppose. According to my census, he's strictly a citizen of Limboville. It's only: why should I waste a perfectly fine ticket? Already paid for? Besides, I've never been to Brazil."

"Just what kind of pills have they been feeding you here? Can't you realize, you're under a criminal indictment. If they catch you jumping bail, they'll throw away the key. Even if you get away with it, you'll never be able to come home."

"Well, so, tough titty. Anyway, home is where you feel at home. I'm still looking."

"No, Holly, it's stupid. You're innocent. You've got to stick it out."

She said, "Rah, team, rah," and blew smoke in my face. She was impressed, however; her eyes were dilated by unhappy visions, as were mine: iron rooms, steel corridors of gradually closing doors. "Oh, screw it," she said, and stabbed out her cigarette. "I have a fair chance they *won't* catch me. Provided *you* keep your *bouche fermez.* Look. Don't despise me, darling." She put her hand over mine and pressed it with sudden immense sincerity. "I haven't much choice. I talked it over with the lawyer: oh, I didn't tell *him* anything *re* Rio—he'd tip the badgers himself, rather than lose his fee, to say nothing of the nickels O.J. put up for bail. Bless O.J.'s heart; but once on the coast I helped him win more than ten thou in a single poker hand: we're square. No, here's the real shake: all the badgers want from me is a couple of free grabs and my services as a state's witness against Sally—nobody has any intention of prosecuting me, they haven't a ghost of a case. Well, I may be rotten to the core, Maude, *but:* testify against a friend I will not. Not if they can prove he doped Sister Kenny. My yardstick is how somebody treats me, and old Sally, all right he wasn't absolutely white with me, say he took a slight advantage, just the same Sally's an okay shooter, and I'd let the fat woman snatch me sooner than help the law-boys pin him down." Tilting her compact mirror above her face, smoothing her lipstick with a crooked pinkie, she said: "And to be honest, that isn't all. Certain shades of limelight wreck a girl's complexion. Even if a jury gave me the Purple Heart, this neighborhood holds no future: they'd still have up every rope from LaRue to Perona's Bar and Grill—take my word, I'd be about as welcome as Mr. Frank E. Campbell. And if you lived off my particular talents, Cookie, you'd understand the kind of bankruptcy I'm describing. Uh, uh, I don't just fancy a fade-out that finds me belly-bumping around Roseland with a pack of West Side hillbillies. While the excellent Madame Trawler sashays her twat in and out of Tiffany's. I couldn't take it. Give me the fat woman any day."

A nurse, soft-shoeing into the room, advised that visiting hours were over. Holly started to complain, and was curtailed by having a thermometer popped in her mouth. But as I took leave, she unstoppered herself to say: "Do me a favor, darling. Call up the *Times,* or whatever you call, and get a list of the fifty richest men in Brazil. I'm *not* kidding. The fifty richest: regardless of race or color. Another favor—poke around my apartment till you find that medal you gave me. The St. Christopher. I'll need it for the trip."

THE SKY WAS RED FRIDAY night, it thundered, and Saturday, departing day, the city swayed in a squall-like downpour. Sharks might have swum through the air, though it seemed improbable a plane could penetrate it.

But Holly, ignoring my cheerful conviction that her flight would not go, continued her preparations—placing, I must say, the chief burden of them on me. For she had decided it would be unwise of her to come near the brownstone. Quite rightly, too: it was under surveillance, whether by police or reporters or other interested parties one couldn't tell—simply a man, sometimes men, who hung around the stoop. So she'd gone from the hospital to a bank and straight then to Joe Bell's bar. "She don't figure she was followed," Joe Bell told me when he came with a message that Holly wanted me to meet her there as soon as possible, a half-hour at most, bringing: "Her jewelry. Her guitar. Toothbrushes and stuff. And a bottle of hundred-year-old brandy: she says you'll find it hid down in the bottom of the dirty-clothes basket. Yeah, oh, and the cat. She wants the cat. But hell," he said, "I don't know we should help her at all. She ought to be protected against herself. Me, I feel like telling the cops. Maybe if I go back and build her some drinks, maybe I can get her drunk enough to call it off."

Stumbling, skidding up and down the fire escape between Holly's apartment and mine, wind-blown and winded and wet to the bone (clawed to the bone as well, for the cat had not looked favorably upon evacuation, especially in such inclement weather) I managed a fast, first-rate job of assembling her going-away belongings. I even found the St. Christopher's medal. Everything was piled on the floor of my room, a poignant pyramid of brassières and dancing slippers and pretty things I packed in Holly's only suitcase. There was a mass left over that I had to put in paper grocery bags. I couldn't think how to carry the cat; until I thought of stuffing him in a pillowcase.

Never mind why, but once I walked from New Orleans to Nancy's Landing, Mississippi, just under five hundred miles. It was a light-hearted lark compared to the journey to Joe Bell's bar. The guitar filled with rain, rain softened the paper sacks, the sacks split and perfume spilled on the pavement, pearls rolled in the gutter: while the wind pushed and the cat scratched, the cat screamed—but worse, I was frightened, a coward to equal José: those storming streets seemed aswarm with unseen presences waiting to trap, imprison me for aiding an outlaw.

The outlaw said: "You're late, Buster. Did you bring the brandy?"

And the cat, released, leaped and perched on her shoulder: his tail swung like a baton conducting rhapsodic music. Holly, too, seemed inhabited by melody, some bouncy *bon voyage* oompahpah. Uncorking the brandy, she said: "This was meant to be part of my hope chest. The idea was, every anniversary we'd have a swig. Thank Jesus I never bought the chest. Mr. Bell, sir, three glasses."

"You'll only need two," he told her. "I won't drink to your foolishness."

The more she cajoled him ("Ah, Mr. Bell. The lady doesn't vanish every day. Won't you toast her?"), the gruffer he was: "I'll have no part of it. If you're going to hell, you'll go on your own. With no further help from me." An inaccurate statement: because seconds after he'd made it a chauffeured limousine drew up outside the bar, and Holly, the first to notice it, put down her brandy, arched her eyebrows, as though she expected to see the District Attorney himself alight. So did I. And when I saw Joe Bell blush, I had to think: by God, he *did* call the police. But then, with burning ears, he announced: "It's nothing. One of them Carey Cadillacs. I hired it. To take you to the airport."

He turned his back on us to fiddle with one of his flower arrangements. Holly said: "Kind, dear Mr. Bell. Look at me, sir."

He wouldn't. He wrenched the flowers from the vase and thrust them at her; they missed their mark, scattered on the floor. "Good-bye," he said; and, as though he were going to vomit, scurried to the men's room. We heard the door lock.

The Carey chauffeur was a worldly specimen who accepted our slapdash luggage most civilly and remained rock-faced when, as the limousine swished uptown through a lessening rain, Holly stripped off her clothes, the riding costume she'd never had a chance to substitute, and struggled into a slim black dress. We didn't talk: talk could have only led to argument; and also, Holly seemed too preoccupied for conversation. She hummed to herself, swigged brandy, she leaned constantly forward to peer out the windows, as if she were hunting an address—or, I decided, taking a last impression of a scene she wanted to remember. It was neither of these. But this: "Stop here," she ordered the driver, and we pulled to the curb of a street in Spanish Harlem. A savage, a garish, a moody neighborhood garlanded with poster-portraits of movie stars and Madonnas. Sidewalk litterings of fruit-rind and rotted newspaper were hurled about by the wind, for the wind still boomed, though the rain had hushed and there were bursts of blue in the sky.

Holly stepped out of the car; she took the cat with her. Cradling him, she scratched his head and asked. "What do you think? This ought to be the right kind of place for a tough guy like you. Garbage cans. Rats galore. Plenty of cat-bums to gang around with. So scram," she said, dropping him; and when he did not move away, instead raised his thug-face and questioned her with yellowish pirate-eyes, she stamped her foot: "I said beat it!" He rubbed against her leg. "I said fuck off!" she shouted, then jumped back in the car, slammed the door, and: "Go," she told the driver. "Go. Go."

I was stunned. "Well, you *are*. You *are* a bitch."

We'd traveled a block before she replied. "I told you. We just met by the river one day: that's all. Independents, both of us. We never made each other any promises. We never—" she said, and her voice collapsed, a tic, an invalid whiteness seized her face. The car had paused for a traffic light. Then she had the door open, she was running down the street; and I ran after her.

But the cat was not at the corner where he'd been left. There was no one, nothing on the street except a urinating drunk and two Negro nuns herding a file of sweet-singing children. Other children emerged from doorways and ladies leaned over their window sills to watch as Holly darted up and down the block, ran back and forth chanting: "You. Cat. Where are you? Here, cat." She kept it up until a bumpy-skinned boy came forward dangling an old tom by the scruff of its neck: "You wants a nice kitty, miss? Gimme a dollar."

The limousine had followed us. Now Holly let me steer her toward it. At the door, she hesitated; she looked past me, past the boy still offering his cat ("Halfa dollar. Two-bits, maybe? Two-bits, it ain't much"), and she shuddered, she had to grip my arm to stand up: "Oh, Jesus God. We did belong to each other. He was mine."

Then I made her a promise, I said I'd come back and find her cat: "I'll take care of him, too. I promise."

She smiled: that cheerless new pinch of a smile. "But what about me?" she said, whispered, and shivered again. "I'm very scared, Buster. Yes, at last. Because it could go on forever. Not knowing what's yours until you've thrown it away. The mean reds, they're nothing. The fat woman, she nothing. This, though: my mouth's so dry, if my life depended on it I couldn't spit." She stepped in the car, sank in the seat. "Sorry, driver. Let's go."

TOMATO'S TOMATO MISSING. And: DRUG-CASE ACTRESS BELIEVED GANGLAND VICTIM. In due time, however, the press reported: FLEEING PLAYGIRL TRACED TO RIO. Apparently no attempt was made by American authorities to recover her, and soon the matter diminished to an occasional gossip-column mention; as a news story, it was revived only once: on Christmas Day, when Sally Tomato died of a heart attack at Sing Sing.

Months went by, a winter of them, and not a word from Holly. The owner of the brownstone sold her abandoned possessions, the white-satin bed, the tapestry, her precious Gothic chair; a new tenant acquired the apartment, his name was Quaintance Smith, and he entertained as many gentlemen callers of a noisy nature as Holly ever had—though in this instance Madame Spanella did not object, indeed she doted on the young man and supplied filet mignon whenever he had a black eye. But in the spring a postcard came: it was scribbled in pencil, and signed with a lipstick kiss: *Brazil was beastly but Buenos Aires the best. Not Tiffany's, but almost. Am joined at the hip with duhvine $enor. Love? Think so. Anyhoo am looking for somewhere to live ($enor has wife, 7 brats) and will let you know address when I know it myself. Mille tendresse.* But the address, if it ever existed, never was sent, which made me sad, there was so much I wanted to write her: that I'd *sold* two stories, had read where the Trawlers were countersuing for divorce, was moving out of the brownstone because it was haunted. But mostly, I wanted to tell about her cat. I had kept my promise; I had found him. It took weeks of after-work roaming through those Spanish Harlem streets, and there were many false alarms—flashes of tiger-striped fur that, upon inspection, were not him. But one day, one cold sunshiny Sunday winter afternoon, it was. Flanked by potted plants and framed by clean lace curtains, he was seated in the window of a warm-looking room: I wondered what his name was, for I was certain he had one now, certain he'd arrived somewhere he belonged. African hut or whatever, I hope Holly has, too.

House of Flowers

OTTILIE SHOULD HAVE BEEN THE happiest girl in Port-au-Prince. As Baby said to her, look at all the things that can be put to your credit. Like what? said Ottilie, for she was vain and preferred compliments to pork or perfume. Like your looks, said Baby: you have a lovely light color, even almost blue eyes, and such a pretty, sweet face—there is no girl on the road with steadier customers, every one of them ready to buy you all the beer you can drink. Ottilie conceded that this was true, and with a smile continued to total her fortunes: I have five silk dresses and a pair of green satin shoes, I have three gold teeth worth thirty thousand francs, maybe Mr. Jamison or someone will give me another bracelet. But, Baby, she sighed, and could not express her discontent.

Baby was her best friend; she had another friend too: Rosita. Baby was like a wheel, round, rolling; junk rings had left green circles on several of her fat fingers, her teeth were dark as burnt tree stumps, and when she laughed you could hear her at sea, at least so the sailors claimed. Rosita, the other friend, was taller than most men, and stronger; at night, with the customers on hand, she minced about, lisping in a silly doll voice, but in the daytime she took spacious, loping strides and spoke out in a military baritone. Both of Ottilie's friends were from the Dominican Republic, and considered it reason enough to feel themselves a cut above the natives of this darker country. It did not concern them that Ottilie was a native. You have brains, Baby told her, and certainly what Baby doted on was a good brain. Ottilie was often afraid that her friends would discover that she could neither read nor write.

The house where they lived and worked was rickety, thin as a steeple, and frosted with fragile, bougainvillaea-vined balconies. Though there was no sign outside, it was called the Champs Elysées. The proprietress, a spinsterish, smothered-looking invalid, ruled from an upstairs room, where she stayed locked away rocking in a rocking chair and drinking ten to twenty Coca-Colas a day. All counted, she had eight ladies working for her; with the exception of Ottilie, no one of them was under thirty. In the evening, when the ladies assembled on the porch, where they chatted and flourished paper fans that beat the air like delirious moths, Ottilie seemed a delightful dreaming child surrounded by older, uglier sisters.

Her mother was dead, her father was a planter who had gone back to France, and she had been brought up in the mountains by a rough peasant family, the sons of whom had each at a young age lain with her in some green and shadowy place. Three years earlier, when she was fourteen, she had come down for the first time to the market in Port-au-Prince. It was a journey of two days and a night, and she'd walked carrying a ten-pound sack of grain; to ease the load she'd let a little of the grain spill out, then a little more, and by the time she had reached the market there was almost none left. Ottilie had cried because she thought of how angry the family would be when she came home without the money for the grain; but these tears were not for long: such a jolly nice man helped her dry them. He bought her a slice of coconut, and took her to see his cousin, who was the proprietress of the Champs Elysées. Ottilie could not believe her good luck; the jukebox music, the satin shoes and joking men were as strange and marvelous as the electric-light bulb in her room, which she never tired of clicking on and off. Soon she had become the most talked-of girl on the road, the proprietress was able to ask double for her, and Ottilie grew vain; she could pose for hours in front of a mirror. It was seldom that she thought of the mountains; and yet, after three years, there was much of the mountains still with her: their winds seemed still to move around her, her hard, high haunches had not softened, nor had the soles of her feet, which were rough as lizard's hide.

When her friends spoke of love, of men they had loved, Ottilie became sulky: How do you feel if you're in love? she asked. Ah, said Rosita with swooning eyes, you feel as though pepper has been sprinkled on your heart, as though tiny fish are swimming in your veins. Ottilie shook her head; if Rosita was telling the truth, then she had never been in love, for she had never felt that way about any of the men who came to the house.

This so troubled her that at last she went to see a *Houngan* who lived in the hills above town. Unlike her friends, Ottilie did not tack Christian pictures on the walls of her room; she did not believe in God, but many gods: of food, light, of death, ruin. The Houngan was in touch with these gods; he kept their secrets on his altar, could hear their voices in the rattle of a gourd, could dispense their power in a potion. Speaking through the gods, the Houngan gave her this message: You must catch a wild bee, he said, and hold it in your closed hand . . . if the bee does not sting, then you will know you have found love.

On the way home she thought of Mr. Jamison. He was a man past fifty, an American connected with an engineering project. The gold bracelets chattering on her wrists were presents from him, and Ottilie, passing a fence snowy with honeysuckle, wondered if after all she was not in love with Mr. Jamison. Black bees festooned the honeysuckle. With a brave thrust of her hand she caught one dozing. Its stab was like a blow that knocked her to her knees; and there she knelt, weeping until it was hard to know whether the bee had stung her hand or her eyes.

IT WAS MARCH, AND EVENTS were leading toward carnival. At the Champs Elysées the ladies were sewing on their costumes; Ottilie's hands were idle, for she had decided not to wear a costume at all. On rah-rah week ends, when drums sounded at the rising moon, she sat at her window and watched with a wandering mind the little bands of singers dancing and drumming their way along the road; she listened to the whistling and the laughter and felt no desire to join in. Somebody would think you were a thousand years old, said Baby, and Rosita said: Ottilie, why don't you come to the cockfight with us?

She was not speaking of an ordinary cockfight. From all parts of the island contestants had arrived bringing their fiercest birds. Ottilie thought she might as well go, and screwed a pair of pearls into her ears. When they arrived the exhibition was already under way; in a great tent a sea-sized crowd sobbed and shouted, while a second crowd, those who could not get in, thronged on the outskirts. Entry was no problem to the ladies from the Champs Elysées: a policeman friend cut a path for them and made room on a bench by the ring. The country people surrounding them seemed embarrassed to find themselves in such stylish company. They looked shyly at Baby's lacquered nails, the rhinestone combs in Rosita's hair, the glow of Ottilie's pearl earrings. However, the fights were exciting, and the ladies were soon forgotten; Baby was annoyed that this should be so, and her eyes rolled about searching for glances in their direction. Suddenly she nudged Ottilie. Ottilie, she said, you've got an admirer: see that boy over there, he's staring at you like you were something cold to drink.

At first she thought he must be someone she knew, for he was looking at her as though she should recognize him; but how could she know him when she'd never known anyone so beautiful, anyone with such long legs, little ears? She could see that he was from the mountains: his straw country hat and the worn-out blue of his thick shirt told her as much. He was a ginger color, his skin shiny as a lemon, smooth as a guava leaf, and the tilt of his head was as arrogant as the black and scarlet bird he held in his hands. Ottilie was used to boldly smiling at men; but now her smile was fragmentary, it clung to her lips like cake crumbs.

Eventually there was an intermission. The arena was cleared, and all who could crowded into it to dance and stamp while an orchestra of drums and strings sang out carnival tunes. It was then that the young man approached Ottilie; she laughed to see his bird perched like a parrot on his shoulder. Off with you, said Baby, outraged that a peasant should ask Ottilie to dance, and Rosita rose menacingly to stand between the young man and her friend. He only smiled, and said: Please, madame, I would like to speak with your daughter. Ottilie felt herself being lifted, felt her hips meet against his to the rhythm of music, and she did not mind at all, she let him lead her into the thickest tangle of dancers. Rosita said: Did you hear that, he thought I was her mother? And Baby, consoling her, grimly said: After all, what do you expect? They're only natives, both of them: when she comes back we'll just pretend we don't know her.

As it happened, Ottilie did not return to her friends. Royal, this was the young man's name, Royal Bonaparte, he told her, had not wanted to dance. We must walk in a quiet place, he said, hold my hand and I will take you. She thought him strange, but did not feel strange with him, for the mountains were still with her, and he was of the mountains. With her hands together, and the iridescent cock swaying on his shoulder, they left the tent and wandered lazily down a white road, then along a soft lane where birds of sunlight fluttered through the greenness of leaning acacia trees.

I have been sad, he said, not looking sad. In my village Juno is a champion, but the birds here are strong and ugly, and if I let him fight I would only have a dead Juno. So I will take him home and say that he won. Ottilie, will you have a dip of snuff?

She sneezed voluptuously. Snuff reminded her of her childhood, and mean as those years had been, nostalgia touched her with its far-reaching wand. Royal, she said, be still a minute, I want to take off my shoes.

Royal himself did not have shoes; his golden feet were slender and airy, and the prints they left were like the track of a delicate animal. He said: How is it that I find you here, in all the world here, where nothing is good, where the rum is bad and the people thieves? Why do I find you here, Ottilie?

Because I must make my way, the same as you, and here there is a place for me. I work in a—oh, kind of hotel.

We have our own place, he said. All the side of a hill, and there at the top of the hill is my cool house. Ottilie, will you come and sit inside it?

Crazy, said Ottilie, teasing him, crazy, and she ran between the trees, and he was after her, his arms out as though he held a net. The bird Juno flared his wings, crowed, flew to the ground. Scratchy leaves and fur of moss thrilled the soles of Ottilie's feet as she lilted through the shade and shadows; abruptly, into a veil of rainbow fern, she fell with a thorn in her heel. She winced when Royal pulled out the thorn; he kissed the place where it had been, his lips moved to her hands, her throat, and it was as though she were among drifting leaves. She breathed the odor of him, the dark, clean smell that was like the roots of things, of geraniums, of heavy trees.

Now that's enough, she pleaded, though she did not feel that this was so: it was only that after an hour of him her heart was about to give out. He was quiet then, his tickly haired head rested above her heart, and shoo she said to the gnats that clustered about his sleeping eyes, shush she said to Juno who pranced around crowing at the sky.

While she lay there, Ottilie saw her old enemy, the bees. Silently, in a line like ants, the bees were crawling in and out of a broken stump that stood not far from her. She loosened herself from Royal's arms, and smoothed a place on the ground for his head. Her hand was trembling as she lay it in the path of the bees, but the first that came along tumbled onto her palm, and when she closed her fingers it made no move to hurt her. She counted ten, just to be sure, then opened her hand, and the bee, in spiraling arcs, climbed the air with a joyful singing.

THE PROPRIETRESS GAVE BABY AND Rosita a piece of advice: Leave her alone, let her go, a few weeks and she will be back. The proprietress spoke in the calm of defeat: to keep Ottilie with her, she'd offered the best room in the house, a new gold tooth, a Kodak, an electric fan, but Ottilie had not wavered, she had gone right on putting her belongings in a cardboard box. Baby tried to help, but she was crying so much that Ottilie had to stop her: it was bound to be bad luck, all those tears falling on a bride's possessions. And to Rosita she said: Rosita, you ought to be glad for me instead of standing there wringing your hands.

It was only two days after the cockfight that Royal shouldered Ottilie's cardboard box and walked her in the dusk toward the mountains. When it was learned that she was no longer at the Champs Elysées many of the customers took their trade elsewhere; others, though remaining loyal to the old place, complained of a gloom in the atmosphere: some evenings there was hardly anyone to buy the ladies a beer. Gradually it began to be felt that Ottilie after all would not come back; at the end of six months the proprietress said: She must be dead.

ROYAL'S HOUSE WAS LIKE A house of flowers; wisteria sheltered the roof, a curtain of vines shaded the windows, lilies bloomed at the door. From the windows one could see far, faint winkings of the sea, as the house was high up a hill; here the sun burned hot but the shadows were cold. Inside, the house was always dark and cool, and the walls rustled with pasted pink and green newspapers. There was only one room; it contained a stove, a teetering mirror on top a marble table, and a brass bed big enough for three fat men.

But Ottilie did not sleep in this grand bed. She was not allowed even to sit upon it, for it was the property of Royal's grandmother, Old Bonaparte. A charred, lumpy creature, bowlegged as a dwarf and bald as a buzzard, Old Bonaparte was much respected for miles around as a maker of spells. There were many who were afraid to have her shadow fall upon them; even Royal was wary of her, and he stuttered when he told her that he'd brought home a wife. Motioning Ottilie to her, the old woman bruised her here and there with vicious little pinches, and informed her grandson that his bride was too skinny: She will die with her first.

Each night the young couple waited to make love until they thought Old Bonaparte had gone to sleep. Sometimes, stretched on the straw moonlit pallet where they slept, Ottilie was sure that Old Bonaparte was awake and watching them. Once she saw a gummy, star-struck eye shining in the dark. There was no use complaining to Royal, he only laughed: What harm was there in an old woman who had seen so much of life wanting to see a little more?

Because she loved Royal, Ottilie put away her grievances and tried not to resent Old Bonaparte. For a long while she was happy; she did not miss her friends or the life in Port-au-Prince; even so, she kept her souvenirs of those days in good repair: with a sewing basket Baby had given her as a wedding gift she mended the silk dresses, the green silk stockings that now she never wore, for there was no place to wear them: only men congregated at the café in the village, at the cockfights. When women wanted to meet they met at the washing stream. But Ottilie was too busy to be lonesome. At daybreak she gathered eucalyptus leaves to start a fire and begin their meals; there were chickens to feed, a goat to be milked, there was Old Bonaparte's whining for attention. Three and four times a day she filled a bucket of drinking water and carried it to where Royal worked in the cane fields a mile below the house. She did not mind that on these visits he was gruff with her: she knew that he was showing off before the other men who worked in the fields, and who grinned at her like split watermelons. But at night, when she had him home, she'd pull his ears and pout that he treated her like a dog until, in the dark of the yard where the fireflies flamed, he would hold her and whisper something to make her smile.

They had been married about five months when Royal began doing the things he'd done before his marriage. Other men went to the café in the evenings, stayed whole Sundays at a cockfight—he couldn't understand why Ottilie should carry on about it; but she said he had no right behaving the way he did, and that if he loved her he wouldn't leave her alone day and night with that mean old woman. I love you, he said, but a man has to have his pleasures too. There were nights when he pleasured himself until the moon was in the middle of the sky; she never knew when he was coming home, and she would lie fretting on the pallet, imagining she could not sleep without his arms around her.

But Old Bonaparte was the real torment. She was about to worry Ottilie out of her mind. If Ottilie was cooking, the terrible old woman was sure to come poking around the stove, and when she did not like what there was to eat she would take a mouthful and spit it on the floor. Every mess she could think of she made: she wet the bed, insisted on having the goat in the room, whatever she touched was soon spilled or broken, and to Royal she complained that a woman who couldn't keep a nice house for her husband was worthless. She was underfoot the whole day, and her red, remorseless eyes were seldom shut; but the worst of it, the thing that finally made Ottilie threaten to kill her, was the old woman's habit of sneaking up from nowhere and pinching her so hard you could see the fingernail marks. If you do that one more time, if you just dare, I'll snatch that knife and cut out your heart! Old Bonaparte knew Ottilie meant it, and though she stopped the pinching, she thought of other jokes: for instance, she made a point of walking all over a certain part of the yard, pretending she did not know that Ottilie had planted a little garden there.

One day two exceptional things happened. A boy came from the village bringing a letter for Ottilie; at the Champs Elysées postcards had once in a while arrived from sailors and other traveling men who had spent pleasant moments with her, but this was the first letter she'd ever received. Since she could not read it, her first impulse was to tear it up: there was no use having it hang around to haunt her. Of course there was a chance that someday she would learn to read; and so she went to hide it in her sewing basket.

When she opened the sewing basket, she made a sinister discovery: there, like a gruesome ball of yarn, was the severed head of a yellow cat. So, the miserable old woman was up to new tricks! She wants to put a spell, thought Ottilie, not in the least frightened. Primly lifting the head by one of its ears, she carried it to the stove and dropped it into a boiling pot: at noon Old Bonaparte sucked her teeth and remarked that the soup Ottilie had made for her was surprisingly tasty.

The next morning, just in time for the midday meal, she found twisting in her basket a small green snake which, chopping fine as sand, she sprinkled into a serving of stew. Each day her ingenuity was tested: there were spiders to bake, a lizard to fry, a buzzard's breast to boil. Old Bonaparte ate several helpings of everything. With a restless glittering her eyes followed Ottilie as she watched for some sign that the spell was taking hold. You don't look well, Ottilie, she said, mixing a little molasses in the vinegar of her voice. You eat like an ant: here now, why don't you have a bowl of this good soup?

Because, answered Ottilie evenly, I don't like buzzard in my soup; or spiders in my bread, snakes in the stew: I have no appetite for such things.

Old Bonaparte understood; with swelling veins and a stricken, powerless tongue, she rose shakily to her feet, then crashed across the table. Before nightfall she was dead.

Royal summoned mourners. They came from the village, from the neighboring hills and, wailing like dogs at midnight, laid siege to the house. Old women beat their heads against the walls, moaning men prostrated themselves: it was the art of sorrow, and those who best mimicked grief were much admired. After the funeral everyone went away, satisfied that they'd done a good job.

Now the house belonged to Ottilie. Without Old Bonaparte's prying and her mess to clean she had more spare time, but she did not know what to do with it. She sprawled on the great brass bed, she loafed in front of the mirror; monotony hummed in her head, and to drive away its fly-buzz sound she would sing the songs she'd learned from the jukebox at the Champs Elysées. Waiting in the twilight for Royal she would remember that at this hour her friends in Port-au-Prince were gossiping on the porch and waiting for the turning headlights of a car; but when she saw Royal ambling up the path, his cane cutter swinging at his side like a crescent moon, she forgot such thoughts and ran with a satisfied heart to meet him.

One night as they lay half-drowsing, Ottilie felt suddenly another presence in the room. Then, gleaming there at the foot of the bed, she saw, as she had seen before, a watching eye; thus she knew what for some time she had suspected: that Old Bonaparte was dead but not gone. Once, when she was alone in the house, she'd heard a laugh, and once again, out in the yard, she'd seen the goat gazing at someone who was not there and twinkling his ears as he did whenever the old woman scratched his skull.

Stop shaking the bed, said Royal, and Ottilie, with a finger raised at the eye, whisperingly asked him if he could not see it. When he replied that she was dreaming, she reached for the eye and screamed at feeling only air. Royal lighted a lamp; he cuddled Ottilie on his lap and smoothed her hair while she told him of the discoveries she'd made in her sewing basket, and of how she had disposed of them. Was it wrong what she'd done? Royal did not know, it was not for him to say, but it was his opinion that she would have to be punished; and why? because the old woman wanted it, because she would otherwise never leave Ottilie in peace: that was the way with haunts.

In accordance with this, Royal fetched a rope the next morning and proposed to tie Ottilie to a tree in the yard: there she was to remain until dark without food or water, and anyone passing would know her to be in a state of disgrace.

But Ottilie crawled under the bed and refused to come out. I'll run away, she whimpered. Royal, if you try to tie me to that old tree I'll run away.

Then I'd have to go and get you, said Royal, and that would be the worse for you.

He gripped her by an ankle and dragged her squealing from under the bed. All the way to the yard she caught at things, the door, a vine, the goat's beard, but none of these would hold her, and Royal was not detained from tying her to the tree. He made three knots in the rope, and went off to work sucking his hand where she had bit him. She hollered to him all the bad words she'd ever heard until he disappeared over the hill. The goat, Juno and the chickens gathered to stare at her humiliation; slumping to the ground, Ottilie stuck out her tongue at them.

BECAUSE SHE WAS ALMOST ASLEEP, Ottilie thought it was a dream when, in the company of a child from the village, Baby and Rosita, wobbling on high heels and carrying fancy umbrellas, tottered up the path calling her name. Since they were people in a dream, they probably would not be surprised to find her tied to a tree.

My God, are you mad? shrieked Baby, keeping her distance as though she feared that indeed this must be the case. Speak to us, Ottilie!

Blinking, giggling, Ottilie said: I'm just happy to see you. Rosita, please untie me so that I can hug you both.

So this is what the brute does, said Rosita, tearing at the ropes. Wait till I see him, beating you and tying you in the yard like a dog.

Oh no, said Ottilie. Royal never beats me. It's just that today I'm being punished.

You wouldn't listen to us, said Baby. And now you see what's come of it. That man has plenty to answer for, she added, brandishing her umbrella.

Ottilie hugged her friends and kissed them. Isn't it a pretty house? she said, leading them toward it. It's like you picked a wagon of flowers and built a house with them: that is what I think. Come in out of the sun. It's cool inside and smells so sweet.

Rosita sniffed as though what she smelled was nothing sweet, and in her well-bottom voice declared that yes, it was better that they stay out of the sun, as it seemed to be affecting Ottilie's head.

It's a mercy that we've come, said Baby, fishing inside an enormous purse. And you can thank Mr. Jamison for that. Madame said you were dead, and when you never answered our letter we thought it must be so. But Mr. Jamison, that's the loveliest man you'll ever know, he hired a car for me and Rosita, your dearest loving friends, to come up here and find out what had happened to our Ottilie. Ottilie, I've got a bottle of rum here in my purse, so get us a glass and we'll all have a round.

The elegant foreign manners and flashing finery of the city ladies had intoxicated their guide, a little boy whose peeking black eyes bobbed at the window. Ottilie was impressed, too, for it was a long time since she'd seen painted lips or smelled bottle perfume, and while Baby poured the rum she got out her satin shoes, her pearl earrings. Dear, said Rosita when Ottilie had finished dressing up, there's no man alive that wouldn't buy you a whole keg of beer; to think of it, a gorgeous piece like you suffering far away from those who love you.

I haven't been suffering so much, said Ottilie. Just sometimes.

Hush now, said Baby. You don't have to talk about it yet. It's all over anyway. Here, dear, let me see your glass again. A toast to old times, and those to be! Tonight Mr. Jamison is going to buy champagne for everybody: Madame is letting him have it at half-price.

Oh, said Ottilie, envying her friends. Well, she wanted to know, what did people say of her, was she remembered?

Ottilie, you have no idea, said Baby; men nobody ever laid eyes on before have come into the place asking where is Ottilie, because they've heard about you way off in Havana and Miami. As for Mr. Jamison, he doesn't even look at us other girls, just comes and sits on the porch drinking by himself.

Yes, said Ottilie wistfully. He was always sweet to me, Mr. Jamison.

Presently the sun was slanting, and the bottle of rum stood three-quarters empty. A thunderburst of rain had for a moment drenched the hills that now, seen through the windows, shimmered like dragonfly wings, and a breeze, rich with the scent of rained-on flowers, roamed the room rustling the green and pink papers on the walls. Many stories had been told, some of them funny, a few that were sad; it was like any night's talk at the Champs Elysées, and Ottilie was happy to be a part of it again.

But it's getting late, said Baby. And we promised to be back before midnight. Ottilie, can we help you pack?

Although she had not realized that her friends expected her to leave with them, the rum stirring in her made it seem a likely assumption, and with a smile she thought: I told him I would go away. Only, she said aloud, it's not like I would have even a week to enjoy myself: Royal will come right down and get me.

Both her friends laughed at this. You're so silly, said Baby. I'd like to see that Royal when some of our men got through with him.

I wouldn't stand for anybody hurting Royal, said Ottilie. Besides, he'd be even madder when we got home.

Baby said: But, Ottilie, you wouldn't be coming back here with him.

Ottilie giggled, and looked about the room as though she saw something invisible to the others. Why, sure I would, she said.

Rolling her eyes, Baby produced a fan and jerked it in front of her face. That's the craziest thing I've ever heard, she said between hard lips. Isn't that the craziest thing you've ever heard, Rosita?

It's that Ottilie's been through so much, said Rosita. Dear, why don't you lie down on the bed while we pack your things?

Ottilie watched as they commenced piling her possessions. They scooped her combs and pins, they wound up her silk stockings. She took off her pretty clothes, as if she were going to put on something finer still; instead, she slipped back into her old dress; then, working quietly, and as though she were helping her friends, she put everything back where it belonged. Baby stamped her foot when she saw what was happening.

Listen, said Ottilie. If you and Rosita are my friends, please do what I tell you: tie me in the yard just like I was when you came. That way no bee is ever going to sting me.

Stinking drunk, said Baby; but Rosita told her to shut up. I think, said Rosita with a sigh, I think Ottilie is in love. If Royal wanted her back, she would go with him, and this being the way things were they might as well go home and say that Madame was right, that Ottilie was dead.

Yes, said Ottilie, for the drama of it appealed to her. Tell them that I am dead.

So they went into the yard; there, with heaving bosoms and eyes as round as the daytime moon scudding above, Baby said she would have no part in tying Ottilie to the tree, which left Rosita to do it alone. On parting, it was Ottilie who cried the most, though she was glad to see them go, for she knew that as soon as they were gone she would not think of them again. Teetering on their high heels down the dips of the path, they turned to wave, but Ottilie could not wave back, and so she forgot them before they were out of sight.

Chewing eucalyptus leaves to sweeten her breath, she felt the chill of twilight twitch the air. Yellow deepened the daytime moon, and roosting birds sailed into the darkness of the tree. Suddenly, hearing Royal on the path, she threw her legs akimbo, let her neck go limp, lolled her eyes far back into their sockets. Seen from a distance, it would look as though she had come to some violent, pitiful end; and, listening to Royal's footsteps quicken to a run, she happily thought: This will give him a good scare.

A Diamond Guitar

THE NEAREST TOWN TO THE prison farm is twenty miles away. Many forests of pine trees stand between the farm and the town, and it is in these forests that the convicts work; they tap for turpentine. The prison itself is in a forest. You will find it there at the end of a red rutted road, barbed wire sprawling like a vine over its walls. Inside, there live one hundred and nine white men, ninety-seven Negroes and one Chinese. There are two sleep houses—great green wooden buildings with tar-paper roofs. The white men occupy one, the Negroes and the Chinese the other. In each sleep house there is one large potbellied stove, but the winters are cold here, and at night with the pines waving frostily and a freezing light falling from the moon the men, stretched on their iron cots, lie awake with the fire colors of the stove playing in their eyes.

The men whose cots are nearest the stove are the important men—those who are looked up to or feared. Mr. Schaeffer is one of these. Mr. Schaeffer—for that is what he is called, a mark of special respect—is a lanky, pulled-out man. He has reddish, silvering hair, and his face is attenuated, religious; there is no flesh to him; you can see the workings of his bones, and his eyes are a poor, dull color. He can read and he can write, he can add a column of figures. When another man receives a letter, he brings it to Mr. Schaeffer. Most of these letters are sad and complaining; very often Mr. Schaeffer improvises more cheerful messages and does not read what is written on the page. In the sleep house there are two other men who can read. Even so, one of them brings his letters to Mr. Schaeffer, who obliges by never reading the truth. Mr. Schaeffer himself does not receive mail, not even at Christmas; he seems to have no friends beyond the prison, and actually he has none there—that is, no particular friend. This was not always true.

One winter Sunday some winters ago Mr. Schaeffer was sitting on the steps of the sleep house carving a doll. He is quite talented at this. His dolls are carved in separate sections, then put together with bits of spring wire; the arms and legs move, the head rolls. When he has finished a dozen or so of these dolls, the Captain of the farm takes them into town, and there they are sold in a general store. In this way Mr. Schaeffer earns money for candy and tobacco.

That Sunday, as he sat cutting out the fingers for a little hand, a truck pulled into the prison yard. A young boy, handcuffed to the Captain of the farm, climbed out of the truck and stood blinking at the ghostly winter sun. Mr. Schaeffer only glanced at him. He was then a man of fifty, and seventeen of those years he'd lived at the farm. The arrival of a new prisoner could not arouse him. Sunday is a free day at the farm, and other men who were moping around the yard crowded down to the truck. Afterward, Pick Axe and Goober stopped by to speak with Mr. Schaeffer.

Pick Axe said, "He's a foreigner, the new one is. From Cuba. But with yellow hair."

"A knifer, Cap'n says," said Goober, who was a knifer himself. "Cut up a sailor in Mobile."

"Two sailors," said Pick Axe. "But just a café fight. He didn't hurt them boys none."

"To cut off a man's ear? You call that not hurtin' him? They give him two years, Cap'n says."

Pick Axe said, "He's got a guitar with jewels all over it."

It was getting too dark to work. Mr. Schaeffer fitted the pieces of his doll together and, holding its little hands, set it on his knee. He rolled a cigarette; the pines were blue in the sundown light, and the smoke from his cigarette lingered in the cold, darkening air. He could see the Captain coming across the yard. The new prisoner, a blond young boy, lagged a pace behind. He was carrying a guitar studded with glass diamonds that cast a starry twinkle, and his new uniform was too big for him; it looked like a Halloween suit.

"Somebody for you, Schaeffer," said the Captain, pausing on the steps of the sleep house. The Captain was not a hard man; occasionally he invited Mr. Schaeffer into his office, and they would talk together about things they had read in the newspaper. "Tico Feo," he said as though it were the name of a bird or a song, "this is Mr. Schaeffer. Do like him, and you'll do right."

Mr. Schaeffer glanced up at the boy and smiled. He smiled at him longer than he meant to, for the boy had eyes like strips of sky—blue as the winter evening—and his hair was as gold as the Captain's teeth. He had a fun-loving face, nimble, clever; and, looking at him, Mr. Schaeffer thought of holidays and good times.

"Is like my baby sister," said Tico Feo, touching Mr.

Schaeffer's doll. His voice with its Cuban accent was soft and sweet as a banana. "She sit on my knee also."

Mr. Schaeffer was suddenly shy. Bowing to the Captain, he walked off into the shadows of the yard. He stood there whispering the names of the evening stars as they opened in flower above him. The stars were his pleasure, but tonight they did not comfort him; they did not make him remember that what happens to us on earth is lost in the endless shine of eternity. Gazing at them—the stars—he thought of the jeweled guitar and its worldly glitter.

It could be said of Mr. Schaeffer that in his life he'd done only one really bad thing: he'd killed a man. The circumstances of that deed are unimportant, except to say that the man deserved to die and that for it Mr. Schaeffer was sentenced to ninety-nine years and a day. For a long while—for many years, in fact—he had not thought of how it was before he came to the farm. His memory of those times was like a house where no one lives and where the furniture has rotted away. But tonight it was as if lamps had been lighted through all the gloomy dead rooms. It had begun to happen when he saw Tico Feo coming through the dusk with his splendid guitar. Until that moment he had not been lonesome. Now, recognizing his loneliness, he felt alive. He had not wanted to be alive. To be alive was to remember brown rivers where the fish run, and sunlight on a lady's hair.

Mr. Schaeffer hung his head. The glare of the stars had made his eyes water.

The sleep house usually is a glum place, stale with the smell of men and stark in the light of two unshaded electric bulbs. But with the advent of Tico Feo it was as though a tropic occurrence had happened in the cold room, for when Mr. Schaeffer returned from his observance of the stars he came upon a savage and garish scene. Sitting cross-legged on a cot, Tico Feo was picking at his guitar with long swaying fingers and singing a song that sounded as jolly as jingling coins. Though the song was in Spanish, some of the men tried to sing it with him, and Pick Axe and Goober were dancing together. Charlie and Wink were dancing too, but separately. It was nice to hear the men laughing, and when Tico Feo finally put aside his guitar, Mr. Schaeffer was among those who congratulated him.

"You deserve such a fine guitar," he said.

"Is diamond guitar," said Tico Feo, drawing his hand over its vaudeville dazzle. "Once I have a one with rubies. But that one is stole. In Havana my sister work in a, how you say, where make guitar; is how I have this one."

Mr. Schaeffer asked him if he had many sisters, and Tico Feo, grinning, held up four fingers. Then, his blue eyes narrowing greedily, he said, "Please, Mister, you give me doll for my two little sister?"

The next evening Mr. Schaeffer brought him the dolls. After that he was Tico Feo's best friend and they were always together. At all times they considered each other.

Tico Feo was eighteen years old and for two years had worked on a freighter in the Caribbean. As a child he'd gone to school with nuns, and he wore a gold crucifix around his neck. He had a rosary too. The rosary he kept wrapped in a green silk scarf that also held three other treasures: a bottle of Evening in Paris cologne, a pocket mirror and a Rand McNally map of the world. These and the guitar were his only possessions, and he would not allow anyone to touch them. Perhaps he prized his map the most. At night, before the lights were turned off, he would shake out his map and show Mr. Schaeffer the places he'd been—Galveston, Miami, New Orleans, Mobile, Cuba, Haiti, Jamaica, Puerto Rico, the Virgin Islands—and the places he wanted to go to. He wanted to go almost everywhere, especially Madrid, especially the North Pole. This both charmed and frightened Mr. Schaeffer. It hurt him to think of Tico Feo on the seas and in far places. He sometimes looked defensively at his friend and thought, "You are just a lazy dreamer."

It is true that Tico Feo was a lazy fellow. After that first evening he had to be urged even to play his guitar. At daybreak when the guard came to rouse the men, which he did by banging a hammer on the stove, Tico Feo would whimper like a child. Sometimes he pretended to be ill, moaned and rubbed his stomach; but he never got away with this, for the Captain would send him out to work with the rest of the men. He and Mr. Schaeffer were put together on a highway gang. It was hard work, digging at frozen clay and carrying croker sacks filled with broken stone. The guard had always to be shouting at Tico Feo, for he spent most of the time trying to lean on things.

Each noon, when the dinner buckets were passed around, the two friends sat together. There were some good things in Mr. Schaeffer's bucket, as he could afford apples and candy bars from the town. He liked giving these things to his friend, for his friend enjoyed them so much, and he thought, "You are growing; it will be a long time until you are a grown man."

Not all the men liked Tico Feo. Because they were jealous, or for more subtle reasons, some of them told ugly stories about him. Tico Feo himself seemed unaware of this. When the men gathered around him, and he played his guitar and sang his songs, you could see that he felt he was loved. Most of the men did feel a love for him; they waited for and depended upon the hour between supper and lights out. "Tico, play your box," they would say. They did not notice that afterward there was a deeper sadness than there had ever been. Sleep jumped beyond them like a jack rabbit, and their eyes lingered ponderingly on the firelight that creaked behind the grating of the stove. Mr. Schaeffer was the only one who understood their troubled feeling, for he felt it too. It was that his friend had revived the brown rivers where the fish run, and ladies with sunlight in their hair.

Soon Tico Feo was allowed the honor of having a bed near the stove and next to Mr. Schaeffer. Mr. Schaeffer had always known that his friend was a terrible liar. He did not listen for the truth in Tico Feo's tales of adventure, of conquests and encounters with famous people. Rather, he took pleasure in them as plain stories, such as you would read in a magazine, and it warmed him to hear his friend's tropic voice whispering in the dark.

Except that they did not combine their bodies or think to do so, though such things were not unknown at the farm, they were as lovers. Of the seasons, spring is the most shattering: stalks thrusting through the earth's winter-stiffened crust, young leaves cracking out on old left-to-die branches, the falling-asleep wind cruising through all the newborn green. And with Mr. Schaeffer it was the same, a breaking up, a flexing of muscles that had hardened.

It was late January. The friends were sitting on the steps of the sleep house, each with a cigarette in his hand. A moon thin and yellow as a piece of lemon rind curved above them, and under its light, threads of ground frost glistened like silver snail trails. For many days Tico Feo had been drawn into himself—silent as a robber waiting in the shadows. It was no good to say to him, "Tico, play your box." He would only look at you with smooth, under-ether eyes.

"Tell a story," said Mr. Schaeffer, who felt nervous and helpless when he could not reach his friend. "Tell about when you went to the race track in Miami."

"I not ever go to no race track," said Tico Feo, thereby admitting to his wildest lie, one involving hundreds of dollars and a meeting with Bing Crosby. He did not seem to care. He produced a comb and pulled it sulkily through his hair. A few days before this comb had been the cause of a fierce quarrel. One of the men, Wink, claimed that Tico Feo had stolen the comb from him, to which the accused replied by spitting in his face. They had wrestled around until Mr. Schaeffer and another man got them separated. "Is my comb. You tell him!" Tico Feo had demanded of Mr. Schaeffer. But Mr. Schaeffer with quiet firmness had said no, it was not his friend's comb—an answer that seemed to defeat all concerned. "Aw," said Wink, "if he wants it so much, Christ's sake, let the sonofabitch keep it." And later, in a puzzled, uncertain voice, Tico Feo had said, "I thought you was my friend." "I am," Mr. Schaeffer had thought; though he said nothing.

"I not go to no race track, and what I said about the widow woman, that is not true also." He puffed up his cigarette to a furious glow and looked at Mr. Schaeffer with a speculating expression. "Say, you have money, Mister?"

"Maybe twenty dollars," said Mr. Schaeffer hesitantly, afraid of where this was leading.

"Not so good, twenty dollar," Tico said, but without disappointment. "No important, we work our way. In Mobile I have my friend Frederico. He will put us on a boat. There will not be trouble," and it was as though he were saying that the weather had turned colder.

There was a squeezing in Mr. Schaeffer's heart; he could not speak.

"Nobody here can run to catch Tico. He run the fastest."

"Shotguns run faster," said Mr. Schaeffer in a voice hardly alive. "I'm too old," he said, with the knowledge of age churning like nausea inside him.

Tico Feo was not listening. "Then, the world. The world, *el mundo,* my friend." Standing up, he quivered like a young horse; everything seemed to draw close to him—the moon, the callings of screech owls. His breath came quickly and turned to smoke in the air. "Should we go to Madrid? Maybe someone teach me to bullfight. You think so, Mister?"

Mr. Schaeffer was not listening either. "I'm too old," he said. "I'm too damned old."

For the next several weeks Tico Feo kept after him—the world, *el mundo,* my friend; and he wanted to hide. He would shut himself in the toilet and hold his head. Nevertheless, he was excited, tantalized. What if it could come true, the race with Tico across the forests and to the sea? And he imagined himself on a boat, he who had never seen the sea, whose whole life had been land-rooted. During this time one of the convicts died, and in the yard you could hear the coffin being made. As each nail thudded into place, Mr. Schaeffer thought, "This is for me, it is mine."

Tico Feo himself was never in better spirits; he sauntered about with a dancer's snappy, gigolo grace, and had a joke for everyone. In the sleep house after supper his fingers popped at the guitar like firecrackers. He taught the men to cry *olé,* and some of them sailed their caps through the air.

When work on the road was finished, Mr. Schaeffer and Tico Feo were moved back into the forests. On Valentine's Day they ate their lunch under a pine tree. Mr. Schaeffer had ordered a dozen oranges from the town and he peeled them slowly, the skins unraveling in a spiral; the juicier slices he gave to his friend, who was proud of how far he could spit the seeds—a good ten feet.

It was a cold beautiful day, scraps of sunlight blew about them like butterflies, and Mr. Schaeffer, who liked working with the trees, felt dim and happy. Then Tico Feo said, "That one, he no could catch a fly in his mouth." He meant Armstrong, a hog-jowled man sitting with a shotgun propped between his legs. He was the youngest of the guards and new at the farm.

"I don't know," said Mr. Schaeffer. He'd watched Armstrong and noticed that, like many people who are both heavy and vain, the new guard moved with a skimming lightness. "He might could fool you."

"I fool him, maybe," said Tico Feo, and spit an orange seed in Armstrong's direction. The guard scowled at him, then blew a whistle. It was the signal for work to begin.

Sometime during the afternoon the two friends came together again; that is, they were nailing turpentine buckets onto trees that stood next to each other. At a distance below them a shallow bouncing creek branched through the woods. "In water no smell," said Tico Feo meticulously, as though remembering something he'd heard. "We run in the water; until dark we climb a tree. Yes, Mister?"

Mr. Schaeffer went on hammering, but his hand was shaking, and the hammer came down on his thumb. He looked around dazedly at his friend. His face showed no reflection of pain, and he did not put the thumb in his mouth, the way a man ordinarily might.

Tico Feo's blue eyes seemed to swell like bubbles, and when in a voice quieter than the wind sounds in the pinetops he said, "Tomorrow," these eyes were all that Mr. Schaeffer could see.

"Tomorrow, Mister?"

"Tomorrow," said Mr. Schaeffer.

The first colors of morning fell upon the walls of the sleep house, and Mr. Schaeffer, who had rested little, knew that Tico Feo was awake too. With the weary eyes of a crocodile he observed the movements of his friend in the next cot. Tico Feo was unknotting the scarf that contained his treasures. First he took the pocket mirror. Its jellyfish light trembled on his face. For a while he admired himself with serious delight, and combed and slicked his hair as though he were preparing to step out to a party. Then he hung the rosary about his neck. The cologne he never opened, nor the map. The last thing he did was to tune his guitar. While the other men were dressing, he sat on the edge of his cot and tuned the guitar. It was strange, for he must have known he would never play it again.

Bird shrills followed the men through the smoky morning woods. They walked single file, fifteen men to a group, and a guard bringing up the rear of each line. Mr. Schaeffer was sweating as though it were a hot day, and he could not keep in marching step with his friend, who walked ahead, snapping his fingers and whistling at the birds.

A signal had been set. Tico Feo was to call, "Time out," and pretend to go behind a tree. But Mr. Schaeffer did not know when it would happen.

The guard named Armstrong blew a whistle, and his men dropped from the line and separated to their various stations. Mr. Schaeffer, though going about his work as best he could, took care always to be in a position where he could keep an eye on both Tico Feo and the guard. Armstrong sat on a stump, a chew of tobacco lopsiding his face, and his gun pointing into the sun. He had the tricky eyes of a cardsharp; you could not really tell where he was looking.

Once another man gave the signal. Although Mr. Schaeffer had known at once that it was not the voice of his friend, panic had pulled at his throat like a rope. As the morning wore on there was such a drumming in his ears he was afraid he would not hear the signal when it came.

The sun climbed to the center of the sky. "He is just a lazy dreamer. It will never happen," thought Mr. Schaeffer, daring a moment to believe this. But "First we eat," said Tico Feo with a practical air as they set their dinner pails on the bank above the creek. They ate in silence, almost as though each bore the other a grudge, but at the end of it Mr. Schaeffer felt his friend's hand close over his own and hold it with a tender pressure.

"Mister Armstrong, time out . . ."

Near the creek Mr. Schaeffer had seen a sweet gum tree, and he was thinking it would soon be spring and the sweet gum ready to chew. A razory stone ripped open the palm of his hand as he slid off the slippery embankment into the water. He straightened up and began to run; his legs were long, he kept almost abreast of Tico Feo, and icy geysers sprayed around them. Back and forth through the woods the shouts of men boomed hollowly like voices in a cavern, and there were three shots, all highflying, as though the guard were shooting at a cloud of geese.

Mr. Schaeffer did not see the log that lay across the creek. He thought he was still running, and his legs thrashed about him; it was as though he were a turtle stranded on its back.

While he struggled there, it seemed to him that the face of his friend, suspended above him, was part of the white winter sky—it was so distant, judging. It hung there but an instant, like a hummingbird, yet in that time he'd seen that Tico Feo had not wanted him to make it, had never thought he would, and he remembered once thinking that it would be a long time before his friend was a grown man. When they found him, he was still lying in the ankle-deep water as though it were a summer afternoon and he were idly floating on the stream.

Since then three winters have gone by, and each has been said to be the coldest, the longest. Two recent months of rain washed deeper ruts in the clay road leading to the farm, and it is harder than ever to get there, harder to leave. A pair of searchlights has been added to the walls, and they burn there through the night like the eyes of a giant owl. Otherwise, there have not been many changes. Mr. Schaeffer, for instance, looks much the same, except that there is a thicker frost of white in his hair, and as the result of a broken ankle he walks with a limp. It was the Captain himself who said that Mr. Schaeffer had broken his ankle attempting to capture Tico Feo. There was even a picture of Mr. Schaeffer in the newspaper, and under it this caption: "Tried to Prevent Escape." At the time he was deeply mortified, not because he knew the other men were laughing, but because he thought of Tico Feo seeing it. But he cut it out of the paper anyway, and keeps it in an envelope along with several clippings pertaining to his friend: a spinster woman told the authorities he'd entered her home and kissed her, twice he was reported seen in the Mobile vicinity, finally it was believed that he had left the country.

No one has ever disputed Mr. Schaeffer's claim to the guitar. Several months ago a new prisoner was moved into the sleep house. He was said to be a fine player, and Mr. Schaeffer was persuaded to lend him the guitar. But all the man's tunes came out sour, for it was as though Tico Feo, tuning his guitar that last morning, had put a curse upon it. Now it lies under Mr. Schaeffer's cot, where its glass diamonds are turning yellow; in the night his hand sometimes searches it out, and his fingers drift across the strings: then, the world.

A Christmas Memory

IMAGINE A MORNING IN LATE November. A coming of winter morning more than twenty years ago. Consider the kitchen of a spreading old house in a country town. A great black stove is its main feature; but there is also a big round table and a fireplace with two rocking chairs placed in front of it. Just today the fireplace commenced its seasonal roar.

A woman with shorn white hair is standing at the kitchen window. She is wearing tennis shoes and a shapeless gray sweater over a summery calico dress. She is small and sprightly, like a bantam hen; but, due to a long youthful illness, her shoulders are pitifully hunched. Her face is remarkable—not unlike Lincoln's, craggy like that, and tinted by sun and wind; but it is delicate too, finely boned, and her eyes are sherry-colored and timid. "Oh my," she exclaims, her breath smoking the windowpane, "it's fruitcake weather!"

The person to whom she is speaking is myself. I am seven; she is sixty-something. We are cousins, very distant ones, and we have lived together—well, as long as I can remember. Other people inhabit the house, relatives; and though they have power over us, and frequently make us cry, we are not, on the whole, too much aware of them. We are each other's best friend. She calls me Buddy, in memory of a boy who was formerly her best friend. The other Buddy died in the 1880's, when she was still a child. She is still a child.

"I knew it before I got out of bed," she says, turning away from the window with a purposeful excitement in her eyes. "The courthouse bell sounded so cold and clear. And there were no birds singing; they've gone to warmer country, yes indeed. Oh, Buddy, stop stuffing biscuit and fetch our buggy. Help me find my hat. We've thirty cakes to bake."

It's always the same: a morning arrives in November, and my friend, as though officially inaugurating the Christmas time of year that exhilarates her imagination and fuels the blaze of her heart, announces: "It's fruitcake weather! Fetch our buggy. Help me find my hat."

The hat is found, a straw cartwheel corsaged with velvet roses out-of-doors has faded: it once belonged to a more fashionable relative. Together, we guide our buggy, a dilapidated baby carriage, out to the garden and into a grove of pecan trees. The buggy is mine; that is, it was bought for me when I was born. It is made of wicker, rather unraveled, and the wheels wobble like a drunkard's legs. But it is a faithful object; springtimes, we take it to the woods and fill it with flowers, herbs, wild fern for our porch pots; in the summer, we pile it with picnic paraphernalia and sugar-cane fishing poles and roll it down to the edge of a creek; it has its winter uses, too: as a truck for hauling firewood from the yard to the kitchen, as a warm bed for Queenie, our tough little orange and white rat terrier who has survived distemper and two rattlesnake bites. Queenie is trotting beside it now.

Three hours later we are back in the kitchen hulling a heaping buggyload of windfall pecans. Our backs hurt from gathering them: how hard they were to find (the main crop having been shaken off the trees and sold by the orchard's owners, who are not us) among the concealing leaves, the frosted, deceiving grass. Caarackle! A cheery crunch, scraps of miniature thunder sound as the shells collapse and the golden mound of sweet oily ivory meat mounts in the milk-glass bowl. Queenie begs to taste, and now and again my friend sneaks her a mite, though insisting we deprive ourselves. "We mustn't, Buddy. If we start, we won't stop. And there's scarcely enough as there is. For thirty cakes." The kitchen is growing dark. Dusk turns the window into a mirror: our reflections mingle with the rising moon as we work by the fireside in the firelight. At last, when the moon is quite high, we toss the final hull into the fire and, with joined sighs, watch it catch flame. The buggy is empty, the bowl is brimful.

We eat our supper (cold biscuits, bacon, blackberry jam) and discuss tomorrow. Tomorrow the kind of work I like best begins: buying. Cherries and citron, ginger and vanilla and canned Hawaiian pineapple, rinds and raisins and walnuts and whiskey and oh, so much flour, butter, so many eggs, spices, flavorings: why, we'll need a pony to pull the buggy home.

But before these purchases can be made, there is the question of money. Neither of us has any. Except for skinflint sums persons in the house occasionally provide (a dime is considered very big money); or what we earn ourselves from various activities: holding rummage sales, selling buckets of hand-picked blackberries, jars of homemade jam and apple jelly and peach preserves, rounding up flowers for funerals and weddings. Once we won seventy-ninth prize, five dollars, in a national football contest. Not that we know a fool thing about football. It's just that we enter any contest we hear about: at the moment our hopes are centered on the fifty-thousand-dollar Grand Prize being offered to name a new brand of coffee (we suggested "A.M."; and, after some hesitation, for my friend thought it perhaps sacrilegious, the slogan "A.M.! Amen!"). To tell the truth, our only *really* profitable enterprise was the Fun and Freak Museum we conducted in a back-yard woodshed two summers ago. The Fun was a stereopticon with slide views of Washington and New York lent us by a relative who had been to those places (she was furious when she discovered why we'd borrowed it); the Freak was a three-legged biddy chicken hatched by one of our own hens. Everybody hereabouts wanted to see that biddy: we charged grownups a nickel, kids two cents. And took in a good twenty dollars before the museum shut down due to the decease of the main attraction.

But one way and another we do each year accumulate Christmas savings, a Fruitcake Fund. These moneys we keep hidden in an ancient bead purse under a loose board under the floor under a chamber pot under my friend's bed. The purse is seldom removed from this safe location except to make a deposit, or, as happens every Saturday, a withdrawal; for on Saturdays I am allowed ten cents to go to the picture show. My friend has never been to a picture show, nor does she intend to: "I'd rather hear you tell the story, Buddy. That way I can imagine it more. Besides, a person my age shouldn't squander their eyes. When the Lord comes, let me see him clear." In addition to never having seen a movie, she has never: eaten in a restaurant, traveled more than five miles from home, received or sent a telegram, read anything except funny papers and the Bible, worn cosmetics, cursed, wished someone harm, told a lie on purpose, let a hungry dog go hungry. Here are a few things she has done, does do: killed with a hoe the biggest rattlesnake ever seen in this county (sixteen rattles), dip snuff (secretly), tame hummingbirds (just try it) till they balance on her finger, tell ghost stories (we both believe in ghosts) so tingling they chill you in July, talk to herself, take walks in the rain, grow the prettiest japonicas in town, know the recipe for every sort of old-time Indian cure, including a magical wart-remover.

Now, with supper finished, we retire to the room in a faraway part of the house where my friend sleeps in a scrap-quilt-covered iron bed painted rose pink, her favorite color. Silently, wallowing in the pleasures of conspiracy, we take the bead purse from its secret place and spill its contents on the scrap quilt. Dollar bills, tightly rolled and green as May buds. Somber fifty-cent pieces, heavy enough to weight a dead man's eyes. Lovely dimes, the liveliest coin, the one that really jingles. Nickels and quarters, worn smooth as creek pebbles. But mostly a hateful heap of bitter-odored pennies. Last summer others in the house contracted to pay us a penny for every twenty-five flies we killed. Oh, the carnage of August: the flies that flew to heaven! Yet it was not work in which we took pride. And, as we sit counting pennies, it is as though we were back tabulating dead flies. Neither of us has a head for figures; we count slowly, lose track, start again. According to her calculations, we have $12.73. According to mine, exactly $13. "I do hope you're wrong, Buddy. We can't mess around with thirteen. The cakes will fall. Or put somebody in the cemetery. Why, I wouldn't dream of getting out of bed on the thirteenth." This is true:

she always spends thirteenths in bed. So, to be on the safe side, we subtract a penny and toss it out the window.

OF THE INGREDIENTS THAT GO into our fruitcakes, whiskey is the most expensive, as well as the hardest to obtain: State laws forbid its sale. But everybody knows you can buy a bottle from Mr. Haha Jones. And the next day, having completed our more prosaic shopping, we set out for Mr. Haha's business address, a "sinful" (to quote public opinion) fish-fry and dancing café down by the river. We've been there before, and on the same errand; but in previous years our dealings have been with Haha's wife, an iodine-dark Indian woman with brassy peroxided hair and a dead-tired disposition. Actually, we've never laid eyes on her husband, though we've heard that he's an Indian too. A giant with razor scars across his cheeks. They call him Haha because he's so gloomy, a man who never laughs. As we approach his café (a large log cabin festooned inside and out with chains of garish-gay naked light bulbs and standing by the river's muddy edge under the shade of river trees where moss drifts through the branches like gray mist) our steps slow down. Even Queenie stops prancing and sticks close by. People have been murdered in Haha's café. Cut to pieces. Hit on the head. There's a case coming up in court next month. Naturally these goings-on happen at night when the colored lights cast crazy patterns and the victrola wails. In the daytime Haha's is shabby and deserted. I knock at the door, Queenie barks, my friend calls: "Mrs. Haha, ma'am? Anyone to home?"

Footsteps. The door opens. Our hearts overturn. It's Mr. Haha Jones himself! And he *is* a giant; he *does* have scars; he *doesn't* smile. No, he glowers at us through

Satan-tilted eyes and demands to know: "What you want with Haha?"

For a moment we are too paralyzed to tell. Presently my friend half-finds her voice, a whispery voice at best: "If you please, Mr. Haha, we'd like a quart of your finest whiskey."

His eyes tilt more. Would you believe it? Haha is smiling! Laughing, too. "Which one of you is a drinkin' man?"

"It's for making fruitcakes, Mr. Haha. Cooking."

This sobers him. He frowns. "That's no way to waste good whiskey." Nevertheless, he retreats into the shadowed café and seconds later appears carrying a bottle of daisy yellow unlabeled liquor. He demonstrates its sparkle in the sunlight and says: "Two dollars."

We pay him with nickels and dimes and pennies. Suddenly, jangling the coins in his hand like a fistful of dice, his face softens. "Tell you what," he proposes, pouring the money back into our bead purse, "just send me one of them fruitcakes instead."

"Well," my friend remarks on our way home, "there's a lovely man. We'll put an extra cup of raisins in *his* cake."

The black stove, stoked with coal and firewood, glows like a lighted pumpkin. Eggbeaters whirl, spoons spin round in bowls of butter and sugar, vanilla sweetens the air, ginger spices it; melting, nose-tingling odors saturate the kitchen, suffuse the house, drift out to the world on puffs of chimney smoke. In four days our work is done. Thirty-one cakes, dampened with whiskey, bask on window sills and shelves.

Who are they for?

Friends. Not necessarily neighbor friends: indeed, the larger share are intended for persons we've met maybe once, perhaps not at all. People who've struck our fancy. Like President Roosevelt. Like the Reverend and Mrs.

J. C. Lucey, Baptist missionaries to Borneo who lectured here last winter. Or the little knife grinder who comes through town twice a year. Or Abner Packer, the driver of the six o'clock bus from Mobile, who exchanges waves with us every day as he passes in a dust-cloud whoosh. Or the young Wistons, a California couple whose car one afternoon broke down outside the house and who spent a pleasant hour chatting with us on the porch (young Mr. Wiston snapped our picture, the only one we've ever had taken). Is it because my friend is shy with everyone *except* strangers that these strangers, and merest acquaintances, seem to us our truest friends? I think yes. Also, the scrapbooks we keep of thank-you's on White House stationery, time-to-time communications from California and Borneo, the knife grinder's penny post cards, make us feel connected to eventful worlds beyond the kitchen with its view of a sky that stops.

Now a nude December fig branch grates against the window. The kitchen is empty, the cakes are gone; yesterday we carted the last of them to the post office, where the cost of stamps turned our purse inside out. We're broke. That rather depresses me, but my friend insists on celebrating—with two inches of whiskey left in Haha's bottle. Queenie has a spoonful in a bowl of coffee (she likes her coffee chicory-flavored and strong). The rest we divide between a pair of jelly glasses. We're both quite awed at the prospect of drinking straight whiskey; the taste of it brings screwed-up expressions and sour shudders. But by and by we begin to sing, the two of us singing different songs simultaneously. I don't know the words to mine, just: *Come on along, come on along, to the dark-town strutters' ball.* But I can dance: that's what I mean to be, a tap dancer in the movies. My dancing shadow rollicks on the walls; our voices rock the chinaware; we giggle: as if unseen hands were tickling us. Queenie rolls on her back, her paws plow the air, something like a grin stretches her black lips. Inside myself, I feel warm and sparky as those crumbling logs, carefree as the wind in the chimney. My friend waltzes round the stove, the hem of her poor calico skirt pinched between her fingers as though it were a party dress: *Show me the way to go home,* she sings, her tennis shoes squeaking on the floor. *Show me the way to go home.*

Enter: two relatives. Very angry. Potent with eyes that scold, tongues that scald. Listen to what they have to say, the words tumbling together into a wrathful tune: "A child of seven! whiskey on his breath! are you out of your mind? feeding a child of seven! must be loony! road to ruination! remember Cousin Kate? Uncle Charlie? Uncle Charlie's brother-in-law? shame! scandal! humiliation! kneel, pray, beg the Lord!"

Queenie sneaks under the stove. My friend gazes at her shoes, her chin quivers, she lifts her skirt and blows her nose and runs to her room. Long after the town has gone to sleep and the house is silent except for the chimings of clocks and the sputter of fading fires, she is weeping into a pillow already as wet as a widow's handkerchief.

"Don't cry," I say, sitting at the bottom of her bed and shivering despite my flannel nightgown that smells of last winter's cough syrup, "don't cry," I beg, teasing her toes, tickling her feet, "you're too old for that."

"It's because," she hiccups, "I *am* too old. Old and funny."

"Not funny. Fun. More fun than anybody. Listen. If you don't stop crying you'll be so tired tomorrow we can't go cut a tree."

She straightens up. Queenie jumps on the bed (where Queenie is not allowed) to lick her cheeks. "I know where we'll find real pretty trees, Buddy. And holly, too. With berries big as your eyes. It's way off in the woods. Farther than we've ever been. Papa used to bring us Christmas trees from there: carry them on his shoulder. That's fifty years ago. Well, now: I can't wait for morning."

Morning. Frozen rime lusters the grass; the sun, round as an orange and orange as hot-weather moons, balances on the horizon, burnishes the silvered winter woods. A wild turkey calls. A renegade hog grunts in the undergrowth. Soon, by the edge of knee-deep, rapid-running water, we have to abandon the buggy. Queenie wades the stream first, paddles across barking complaints at the swiftness of the current, the pneumonia-making coldness of it. We follow, holding our shoes and equipment (a hatchet, a burlap sack) above our heads. A mile more: of chastising thorns, burs and briers that catch at our clothes; of rusty pine needles brilliant with gaudy fungus and molted feathers. Here, there, a flash, a flutter, an ecstasy of shrillings remind us that not all the birds have flown south. Always, the path unwinds through lemony sun pools and pitch vine tunnels. Another creek to cross: a disturbed armada of speckled trout froths the water round us, and frogs the size of plates practice belly flops; beaver workmen are building a dam. On the farther shore, Queenie shakes herself and trembles. My friend shivers, too: not with cold but enthusiasm. One of her hat's ragged roses sheds a petal as she lifts her head and inhales the pine-heavy air. "We're almost there; can you smell it, Buddy?" she says, as though we were approaching an ocean.

And, indeed, it is a kind of ocean. Scented acres of holiday trees, prickly-leafed holly. Red berries shiny as Chinese bells: black crows swoop upon them screaming. Having stuffed our burlap sacks with enough greenery and crimson to garland a dozen windows, we set about choosing a tree.

"It should be," muses my friend, "twice as tall as a boy. So a boy can't steal the star." The one we pick is twice as tall as me. A brave handsome brute that survives thirty hatchet strokes before it keels with a creaking rending cry. Lugging it like a kill, we commence the long trek out. Every few yards we abandon the struggle, sit down and pant. But we have the strength of triumphant huntsmen; that and the tree's virile, icy perfume revive us, goad us on. Many compliments accompany our sunset return along the red clay road to town; but my friend is sly and noncommittal when passers-by praise the treasure perched in our buggy: what a fine tree and where did it come from? "Yonderways," she murmurs vaguely. Once a car stops and the rich mill owner's lazy wife leans out and whines: "Giveya two-bits cash for that ol' tree." Ordinarily my friend is afraid of saying no; but on this occasion she promptly shakes her head: "We wouldn't take a dollar." The mill owner's wife persists. "A dollar, my foot! Fifty cents. That's my last offer. Goodness, woman, you can get another one." In answer, my friend gently reflects: "I doubt it. There's never two of anything."

Home: Queenie slumps by the fire and sleeps till tomorrow, snoring loud as a human.

A TRUNK IN THE ATTIC contains: a shoebox of ermine tails (off the opera cape of a curious lady who once rented a room in the house), coils of frazzled tinsel gone gold with age, one silver star, a brief rope of dilapidated, undoubtedly dangerous candy-like light bulbs. Excellent decorations, as far as they go, which isn't far enough: my friend wants our tree to blaze "like a Baptist window," droop with weighty snows of ornament. But we can't afford the made-in-Japan splendors at the five-and-dime. So we do what we've always done: sit for days at the kitchen table with scissors and crayons and stacks of colored paper. I make sketches and my friend cuts them out: lots of cats, fish too (because they're easy to draw), some apples, some watermelons, a few winged angels devised from saved-up sheets of Hershey-bar tin foil. We use safety pins to attach these creations to the tree; as a final touch, we sprinkle the branches with shredded cotton (picked in August for this purpose). My friend, surveying the effect, clasps her hands together. "Now honest, Buddy. Doesn't it look good enough to eat?" Queenie tries to eat an angel.

After weaving and ribboning holly wreaths for all the front windows, our next project is the fashioning of family gifts. Tie-dye scarves for the ladies, for the men a home-brewed lemon and licorice and aspirin syrup to be taken "at the first Symptoms of a Cold and after Hunting." But when it comes time for making each other's gift, my friend and I separate to work secretly. I would like to buy her a pearl-handled knife, a radio, a whole pound of chocolate-covered cherries (we tasted some once, and she always swears: "I could live on them, Buddy, Lord yes I could—and that's not taking His name in vain"). Instead, I am building her a kite. She would like to give me a bicycle (she's said so on several million occasions: "If only I could, Buddy. It's bad enough in life to do without something *you* want; but confound it, what gets my goat is not being able to give somebody something you want *them* to have. Only one of these days I will, Buddy. Locate you a bike. Don't ask how. Steal it, maybe"). Instead, I'm fairly certain that she is building me a kite—the same as last year, and the year before: the year before that we exchanged slingshots. All of which is fine by me. For we are champion kite-fliers who study the wind like sailors; my friend, more accomplished than I, can get a kite aloft when there isn't enough breeze to carry clouds.

Christmas Eve afternoon we scrape together a nickel and go to the butcher's to buy Queenie's traditional gift, a good gnawable beef bone. The bone, wrapped in funny paper, is placed high in the tree near the silver star. Queenie knows it's there. She squats at the foot of the tree staring up in a trance of greed: when bedtime arrives she refuses to budge. Her excitement is equaled by my own. I kick the covers and turn my pillow as though it were a scorching summer's night. Somewhere a rooster crows: falsely, for the sun is still on the other side of the world.

"Buddy, are you awake?" It is my friend, calling from her room, which is next to mine; and an instant later she is sitting on my bed holding a candle. "Well, I can't sleep a hoot," she declares. "My mind's jumping like a jack rabbit. Buddy, do you think Mrs. Roosevelt will serve our cake at dinner?" We huddle in the bed, and she squeezes my hand I-love-you. "Seems like your hand used to be so much smaller. I guess I hate to see you grow up. When you're grown up, will we still be friends?" I say always. "But I feel so bad, Buddy. I wanted so bad to give you a bike. I tried to sell my cameo Papa gave me. Buddy—" she hesitates, as though embarrassed—"I made you another kite." Then I confess that I made her one, too; and we laugh. The candle burns too short to hold. Out it goes, exposing the starlight, the stars spinning at the window like a visible caroling that slowly, slowly daybreak silences. Possibly we doze; but the beginnings of dawn splash us like cold water: we're up, wide-eyed and wandering while we wait for others to waken. Quite deliberately my friend drops a kettle on the kitchen floor. I tap-dance in front of closed doors. One by one the household emerges, looking as though they'd like to kill us both; but it's Christmas, so they can't. First, a gorgeous breakfast: just everything you can imagine—from flapjacks and fried squirrel to hominy grits and honey-in-the-comb. Which puts everyone in a good humor except my friend and I. Frankly, we're so impatient to get at the presents we can't eat a mouthful.

Well, I'm disappointed. Who wouldn't be? With socks, a Sunday school shirt, some handkerchiefs, a hand-me-down sweater and a year's subscription to a religious magazine for children. *The Little Shepherd.* It makes me boil. It really does.

My friend has a better haul. A sack of Satsumas, that's her best present. She is proudest, however, of a white wool shawl knitted by her married sister. But she *says* her favorite gift is the kite I built her. And it *is* very beautiful; though not as beautiful as the one she made me, which is blue and scattered with gold and green Good Conduct stars; moreover, my name is painted on it, "Buddy."

"Buddy, the wind is blowing."

The wind is blowing, and nothing will do till we've run to a pasture below the house where Queenie has scooted to bury her bone (and where, a winter hence, Queenie will be buried, too.) There, plunging through the healthy waist-high grass, we unreel our kites, feel them twitching at the string like sky fish as they swim into the wind. Satisfied, sun-warmed, we sprawl in the grass and peel Satsumas and watch our kites cavort. Soon I forget the socks and hand-me-down sweater. I'm as happy as if we'd already won the fifty-thousand-dollar Grand Prize in that coffee-naming contest.

"My, how foolish I am!" my friend cries, suddenly alert,

like a woman remembering too late she has biscuits in the oven. "You know what I've always thought?" she asks in a tone of discovery, and not smiling at me but a point beyond. "I've always thought a body would have to be sick and dying before they saw the Lord. And I imagined that when He came it would be like looking at the Baptist window: pretty as colored glass with the sun pouring through, such a shine you don't know it's getting dark. And it's been a comfort: to think of that shine taking away all the spooky feeling. But I'll wager it never happens. I'll wager at the very end a body realizes the Lord has already shown Himself. That things as they are"—her hand circles in a gesture that gathers clouds and kites and grass and Queenie pawing earth over her bone—"just what they've always seen, was seeing Him. As for me, I could leave the world with today in my eyes."

THIS IS OUR LAST CHRISTMAS together.

Life separates us. Those who Know Best decide that I belong in a military school. And so follows a miserable succession of bugle-blowing prisons, grim reveille-ridden summer camps. I have a new home too. But it doesn't count. Home is where my friend is, and there I never go.

And there she remains, puttering around the kitchen. Alone with Queenie. Then alone. ("Buddy dear," she writes in her wild hard-to-read script, "yesterday Jim Macy's horse kicked Queenie bad. Be thankful she didn't feel much. I wrapped her in a Fine Linen sheet and rode her in the buggy down to Simpson's pasture where she can be with all her Bones . . ."). For a few Novembers she continues to bake her fruitcakes single-handed; not as many, but some: and, of course, she always sends me "the best of the batch." Also, in every letter she encloses a dime wadded in toilet paper: "See a picture show and write me the story." But gradually in her letters she tends to confuse me with her other friend, the Buddy who died in the 1880's; more and more thirteenths are not the only days she stays in bed: a morning arrives in November, a leafless birdless coming of winter morning, when she cannot rouse herself to exclaim: "Oh my, it's fruitcake weather!"

And when that happens, I know it. A message saying so merely confirms a piece of news some secret vein had already received, severing from me an irreplaceable part of myself, letting it loose like a kite on a broken string. That is why, walking across a school campus on this particular December morning, I keep searching the sky. As if I expected to see, rather like hearts, a lost pair of kites hurrying toward heaven.

ALSO BY TRUMAN CAPOTE

ANSWERED PRAYERS

Although Truman Capote's last novel was unfinished at the time of his death, its surviving portions offer a devastating group portrait of the high and low society of his time. As it follows the career of a writer of uncertain parentage and omnivorous erotic tastes, *Answered Prayers* careens from a louche bar in Tangiers to a banquette at La Côte Basque, from literary salons to high-priced whorehouses. It takes in calculating beauties and sadistic husbands along with such real-life supporting characters as Colette, the Duchess of Windsor, Montgomery Clift, and Tallulah Bankhead. Above all, this malevolently funny book displays Capote at his most relentlessly observant and murderously witty.

Fiction/Literature

THE COMPLETE STORIES OF TRUMAN CAPOTE

A landmark collection that brings together Truman Capote's life's work in the form he called his "great love," *The Complete Stories* confirms Capote's status as a master of the short story. This first-ever compendium features a never-before-published 1950 story, "The Bargain," as well as an introduction by Reynolds Price. Ranging from the gothic South to the chic East Coast, from rural children to aging urban sophisticates, all the unforgettable places and people of Capote's oeuvre are here, in stories as elegant as they are heartfelt, as haunting as they are compassionate.

Fiction/Literature/Short Stories

THE GRASS HARP

Set on the outskirts of a small Southern town, *The Grass Harp* tells the story of three endearing misfits—an orphaned boy and two whimsical old ladies—who one day take up residence in a tree house. As they pass sweet yet hazardous hours in a china tree, *The Grass Harp* manages to convey all the pleasures and responsibilities of freedom. But most of all it teaches us about the sacredness of love, "that love is a chain of love, as nature is a chain of life." This volume also includes Capote's *A Tree of Night and Other Stories*, which the *Washington Post* called "unobtrusively beautiful . . . a superlative book."

Fiction/Literature

IN COLD BLOOD

On November 15, 1959, in the small town of Holcomb, Kansas, four members of the Clutter family were savagely murdered by blasts from a shotgun held a few inches from their faces. There was no apparent motive for the crime, and there were almost no clues. As Truman Capote reconstructs the murder and the investigation that led to the capture, trial, and execution of the killers, he generates both mesmerizing suspense and astonishing empathy. *In Cold Blood* is a work that transcends its moment, yielding poignant insights into the nature of American violence.

Nonfiction/Literature

MUSIC FOR CHAMELEONS

In these gems of reportage Truman Capote takes true stories and real people and renders them with the stylistic brio we expect from great fiction. Here we encounter an exquisitely preserved Creole aristocrat sipping absinthe in her Martinique salon; an enigmatic killer who sends his victims announcements of their forthcoming demise; and a proper Connecticut householder with a ruinous obsession for a twelve-year-old he has never met. And we meet Capote himself, who, whether he is smoking with his cleaning lady or trading sexual gossip with Marilyn Monroe, remains one of the most elegant, malicious, yet compassionate writers to train his eye on the social fauna of his time.

Nonfiction/Literature

OTHER VOICES, OTHER ROOMS

Truman Capote's first novel is a story of almost supernatural intensity and inventiveness, an audacious foray into the mind of a sensitive boy as he seeks out the grown-up enigmas of love and death in the ghostly landscape of the deep South. At the age of twelve, Joel Knox is summoned to meet the father who abandoned him at birth. But when Joel arrives at the decaying mansion in Skully's Landing, his father is nowhere in sight. What he finds instead is a sullen stepmother who delights in killing birds; an uncle with the face—and heart—of a debauched child; and a fearsome little girl named Idabel who may offer him the closest thing he has ever known to love.

Fiction/Literature

TOO BRIEF A TREAT

The Letters of Truman Capote

Edited by Gerald Clarke

The private letters of Truman Capote, lovingly assembled here for the first time by acclaimed Capote biographer Gerald Clarke, provide an intimate, unvarnished portrait of one of the twentieth century's most colorful and fascinating literary figures. Capote was an inveterate letter writer. He wrote letters as he spoke: emphatically, spontaneously, and passionately. Spanning more than four decades, his letters are the closest thing we have to a Capote autobiography, showing us the uncannily self-possessed naïf who jumped headlong into the post–World War II New York literary scene; the more mature Capote of the 1950s; the Capote of the early 1960s, immersed in the research and writing of *In Cold Blood*; and Capote later in life, as things seem to be unraveling. With cameos by a veritable who's who of twentieth-century glitterati, *Too Brief a Treat* shines a spotlight on the life and times of an incomparable American writer.

Biography/Letters